CRAPPY TO HAPPY

To Michael

Who serves with love & grace!

Randy Peyser

CRAPPY TO HAPPY

Small Steps to Big Happiness NOW!

Randy Peyser

Red Wheel
Boston, MA / York Beach, ME

First published in 2002
by Red Wheel/Weiser, LLC
York Beach, ME
With offices at:
368 Congress St. Boston, MA 02210
www.redwheelweiser.com

Library of Congress Cataloging-in-Publication Data
Peyser, Randy.
Crappy to happy : small steps tp big happiness now! / Randy Peyser.
p. cm.
ISBN 1-59003-025-7
1. Happiness. 2. Conduct of life. 3. New Age movement. I. Title
BJ1481 .P44 2002
170'.44--dc21
2002001027

Typeset in Perpetua

Printed in Canada

09 08 07 06 05 04 03 02
8 7 6 5 4 3 2 1

In memory of Ida Fourman,
my grandmother and guiding star

Contents

Acknowledgments

Did you ever notice when a new author publishes her first book, she'll thank everyone in the universe for supporting her in the process? Well, this is my first book, so here it goes!

My love and thanks go to:

Carol Kunz, for her cheerleading and unceasing belief in me.

My mom, Harriet, who says she is proud of me because of who I am, not because of what I do or don't do.

My dad, Marvin, who still does my taxes for me.

Burt Lehrenbaum, my champion with a red pen, who's able to leap tall manuscripts in a single bound.

Karen Emerick, who made me eliminate over 300 unnecessary "buts" and "thats" from the manuscript.

Oshara, who cracks me up with her unceasing one-liners.

Bonnie Britt, Bob Warden, Jason Leen, Art Gottlieb, Sally Richards, and Kare Anderson, advisors along the way.

My network of angels made visible:—Rev. Delorise Lucas, Jill Lublin, Stormin' Norman Mosher, ShaunDarius Gottlieb, Aileen Malmgren, MaryEllen Angelscribe, Maxine Steingold, Debi Nunes, Camille Kurtz, the folks at the Center for Attitudinal Healing in Sausalito, California, and everyone else who knows they are included here.

Thank you to all who have allowed me to share their words or stories with you—Oshara, Mom, Dad, Ted & Roxane Peyser, Carol Kunz, Mary Kelly, Elizabeth Good, Elizabeth Powers, Kathryn Beyers, Debi Nunes, Elissa Gae, Alan, Mahima, Martha

Colburn, Kristan Leatherman, Mark Libowitz, Barbara Brennan, John Gray, Esther Hicks, Matt Garrigan and the *Village Voice.*

And special thanks to Robyn Heisey and Red Wheel/Weiser for catapulting me into fame and fortune with my first book! Wink. Wink.

Lastly, I acknowledge that tiny voice inside me which guides me ever on my way.

What tiny voice? It's louder than a boom box.

Okay, I'll rewrite it. And lastly, I acknowledge that booming voice inside me which guides my life.

What about this voice? Are you hearing voices again?

No, no. It's not what you think. I'm tuning into a greater part of my Self. As I learn how to listen to this part, I'm able to make decisions that lead me to greater and greater happiness. But right now, let me finish the Acknowledgments page so readers can get to the book, okay?

Okey-dokey. It's your book.

Thanks!

Introduction

Based on how you feel right this moment, if you were one of Snow White's seven dwarves, which one would you be? Would you choose "Happy?" The chances are probably slim. Let's update *Snow White* to accurately reflect our current lifestyles.

Hi-ho. Hi-ho. Here comes Overworkey, No-Timey, Un-Happy, Sicky, Stressy, Depressy, and Confusey. Oh, look, and there are the new baby twins, Whiny and Complainy. Isn't this more realistic?

Our happiness is primarily circumstantial. Something wonderful happens and we are flying over the rainbow. Something sad or stressful happens and we dive into the deep dark pit of no return.

What if your happiness had nothing to do with the outer circumstances of your life? What if it was something you just started feeling more and more in each moment regardless of your daily drama?

Is it really possible, or is this just some clever ploy to promote a remake of *Snow White*?

A Testimonial from a True Believer

Yes, it is possible to have an increasingly happier Now. In fact, right this moment I'm having a happier Now. Hold on. Don't get jealous. Listen to my current scenario and then decide if you want to be first in line to change places with me. I no longer have a job to fall back on and I'm not in a relationship.

My bank account is dwindling down to pennies and I have a rinky-dink car with more holes than a golf course. My happiness is obviously not circumstantial—yet I'm truly happier than I've ever been.

And I'm not going through life with a "nothing matters, therefore, I'm happy" attitude, either. I'm experiencing a happier Now because the quality of my Now—how I think, feel, and act in this moment—feels better than it ever did before.

Do I still have moments when I could lick paint off the floor because I feel so low? (Kids, don't try this at home). Yes. The key, however, is I am able to pick myself up and get back on track a lot quicker than I used to.

No one finds happiness in two seconds. At least I didn't. It took a forty-year experiment called, "My Life: Figure It Out," to learn the steps that brought me to this place. Actually, it wasn't about getting it all figured out. Rather, it was about getting it all figured in. Somehow this all figures into this crazy world I call my reality.

Let me be clear. I am not the crazy one. I'm the insightful one, the deep daughter, the person who searches for wisdom and guidance from Spirit, the creator of art and music, the doer of dishes who does not like to vacuum.

I am Truth's daughter.
Hope's sister.
Faith's mother.
Beauty's cousin.
Joy's sister-in-law.
Love's grandmother and
Grace's second cousin once-removed.
(Where do they put people when they "once remove" them?
Alas, this is a question for another time.)

Can You Create a Happier Now by Reading This Book?

I offer you, dear reader, a selection of personal stories as to how I created greater happiness in my life.

Following each story, you will find a page of numbered steps that invite your action or introspection. These "Steps To Happiness NOW!" can help bring you into a more present and happier state of being should you choose to incorporate them into your life.

Are you ready? Have your water bottle and some trail mix? (Get the kind that doesn't sulfur the dried apricots.) Also, pack an inquisitive attitude and an open mind. It's time to go explore the present moment!

SECTION 1

IT'S MY LIFE. TRUE OR FALSE?

Censor the Censor Within

- This section is about discovering and gently removing (or hacking away) the blocks to true self-expression that can lead to greater happiness.

- How many times have you stopped yourself from doing something because you were concerned about what others might think or because you wanted to be perfect on the first try?

- When you allow your inner being to flourish without judgment, you will naturally tap a wellspring of creativity and joy.

- As we explore this first section, we're going to discover our greater personal truths, find the freedom to take risks, and overrule the judge and jury in our heads which say, "Nyah, nyah, you can't do it, you never could."

The Not So Near, Near-Death Experience

It's Story Time...

I am in the middle of having a not so near, near-death experience. Scenes from my life are flashing before me, but I am not dying. It's just that my life has gone to the dumpster. Half of it I carted there myself, the rest got tossed in spite of me. At the bottom of the dumpster sits:

1961

Victimization.

It is my first day at summer Girl Scout Camp. I am ordered to clean out the latrines. I guess that is why we are called, "Brownies."

1962

Envy.

I am squeaking out, "Hey, There, Georgie Girl," on a poorly played clarinet while eyeing the lucky kids who get to play the drums in the school band.

1965

Fear.

Mommy and Daddy are fighting almost every day. I notice our family is nothing like Beaver's.

1972

Morbidity.

I am in high school. I think I am gay. I am writing poetry about angst, death, and peace—in that order.

1973

Relief.

I can play the theme song from *MASH* on my guitar, which promises me "suicide is painless."

1975

Freedom.

I am in college. How did I ever live before overalls and flannel shirts?

1977

Rebellion.

Using a razor, I carefully design women's symbols from the massive hair growth on my unshaved legs.

1980

Challenge.

Collective living. I wonder how many people I can sleep with in nine months? (The answer is nine and I only get one STD!)

1983

Disappointment.

I decide I am not gay and find Mr. Right. Ding-dong, the bells are gonna chime. Ding-damn, he decides he's not "good enough for me" and leaves.

1984
Expectation.
I move to the West Coast with a 900-pound broken heart in tow. The Golden Gate Bridge is supposed to be gold, not picnic-table red. Isn't it?

1986
Frustration.
The library accuses me of never returning a book that I returned. Should missing books be featured on milk cartons?

1987
Illness.
My body goes whacka-whacka with Epstein-Barr Virus and Cytomegalovirus for a couple of years. Walls give me something to lean against so I can make it to the front door for my home-delivered meals.

1994
Meltdown.
I am in a stress-filled job and an on-again-off-again relationship. Both dissolve at the same time a very dear former employer commits suicide.

1996
Confusion.
I am the editor-in-chief of a national magazine. One day, my boss gives me a stock bonus as a "thank-you" for my work. Two weeks later, I am laid off.

1997
Amazement.

I am supposed to be married with kids by now. Instead, I am in my forties and looking for a wiener dog.

1998
Insight.
Everyone I know named Elizabeth is in a long-term relationship. Maybe I should change my name to Elizabeth.

1999
Concern.
I am single. I have no retirement savings. I want to save the world; however, I can't even seem to save myself. In this second, I have no definition. Am I just a "New Age Flake" like my brother says?

***

"What am I doing?" is the most frequent question I ask as I let go of my most recent job and relationship. The answer always comes back the same: "You are being true to yourself. You are living your Truth."

But I am falling into nothing. "This is crazy," I say to myself. "No job, no security, saying good-bye to someone who loves me, whom I love."

Then my inner voice pipes in. "I am not at peace. There is something different that I need." It is up to me to find out what that is.

In the process of letting go of all that is no longer me, I am becoming an expert at grieving, at saying "good-bye" to the old me. So many tears, so much grief. It feels like industrial strength let-go. It is not pretty and it is not much fun, either. Maybe I should take some steps to create a new life right now.

"Okay, let's get a spiffy new job. Resumes, resumes, resumes. Kick 'em out there. You're qualified. You can do any number of things really, really well. You can get some big, important job and do something even bigger and more important for the world. Yahoo, go for it, girl!"

Nothing happens. Nothing. Another big pep talk. "Kick out more resumes." Crank. Crank. Crank. Nothing. I look at the bulletin board over my work desk. Leads, leads, and more leads, all leading nowhere.

"STOP! Enough already. It's not happening. My life is not happening."

It doesn't seem to matter what I do right now. Doing and doing and more doing has only led to a pile of doo-doo. It's just not happening. Maybe I am not supposed to be working right now. I've worked very hard for a long time. Perhaps it's time to just stop. Stop everything.

An Experiment

I decide to try an experiment. For the next two weeks, I am only going to do what I feel "pulled" to do. I'll just tune in to Spirit and listen to my Self. I will follow my intuition and only do what I feel moved to do in every moment.

So I listen.

In the morning I wake up, shower, and eat some breakfast. "Okay, Self. What now?" I tune in. "Drum. Go hit some drums." I have sixteen drums that keep me happily occupied for the next hour.

"What now?" Sadness washes over me. I need to sit and cry. Let out some of the spillover. After all, I am saying good-bye to something very precious. Me—the old me.

For the next hour, I let the tears fall. I pound the bed. I grab a teddy bear and hide under the pillow. I keep breathing and the breath pushes the emotions out. My emotions are very fluid. I let out whatever feelings are in me, a combination of anger, grief, and sadness, and maybe a touch of fear, and then I relax.

Okay, that took up a good chunk of time and I released a lot of the build-up. "What now?" I keep listening and following the moment. "Silk. Go play with silk." I go off to paint something.

Afterwards, I eat some lunch and am ready for the afternoon. "What now?"

"Sit. Do nothing."

I sit. And do nothing.

"Listen. Just listen and be. No need to go anywhere, or do anything. Just be." I sit for a long time. Just breathing. Just listening. Just being.

For two weeks, I keep following my intuitive flow. I'm only doing what I want to be doing in each moment, but I am still not a happy camper. What is going on in my mind?

Chatter. Confusion. I am getting caught in my train of thought. It sounds something like, "Maybe I'm supposed to move out of the area. Maybe I'm supposed to be down in Campbell." I have friends there and already feel like a part of the community. "But I don't want to be one and a half hours from where I am now."

Then I tell myself something big and important. It's so important that I'm going to capitalize it.—"QUIT FUTURE-FEARING. It's not happening now. Be in this moment. If you're supposed to move to Campbell, you'll move to Campbell when it's time—but that's not happening in this moment. Be in this moment. You don't have to worry about moving. It's not happening now. Just be in this moment happening right now."

I start to settle into a deeper place of quiet in my soul, and each day begins to feel more and more like a living meditation.

I try to catch myself every time I start future-fearing about work, money, relationships, or moving, and focus back on the present.

So here I am in the present moment, deciding what I want to happen now. Right now. In this now.

I start playing with some materials. Feathers, fur, stones. I start arranging the feathers on a giant straw fishing tray, splashes of iridescent blue, shimmering purples, shrieking reds, brilliant orange-golds, and soft browns.

My friend Debi has given me all these exquisite feathers. She works with birds from all over the world. When she cleans their pens, she picks up the feathers that have molted. She works in silence, and this routine has become her daily meditation.

I think about how a feather falls off a bird. The bird simply molts when it's time to molt. There is no pain involved. It just lets go of something it no longer needs when it's time to let go. Like the leaves of an autumn maple, the feathers fall off gently, easily, as part of a natural cycle. Why do I make it so hard for myself when I know it is my time to let go?

I keep working. The fur. The beautiful fur. I don't believe in hurting or killing animals for their fur. The furs I use come from ratty, fifty-year-old coats, recycled from flea market stalls. I see it as a way of honoring the fur-beings from the past.

The tiny, round, smooth stones. Gray, jade, burnt red, ochre, tan. Picked up by a friend's uncle who enjoyed walking on the beach in meditation. Given to me after the uncle died. Stored in an onyx box. I've had them for ten years. Their time is now.

I work in meditation. Silently. Listening. Fur, feathers, stone, straw, and glue. I find a comb of my grandmother's, a beautiful golden hair comb with a tiny pink flower at its center. It wants to join the piece as well.

I pour the stones onto the fishing tray. A penny tumbles out and wedges itself between the stones. The part that sticks out reads, "In God We Trust." I decide to keep it there.

I spend hours in silent meditation working on it. The eye of a peacock feather graces its center. I finish the piece and I am pleased. Its title comes to me. It is, "The Mandala of Being." Mandala—the circle that connects all. Every bit of it done in meditation. The collecting of the feathers and stones, the arrangement of the materials on the fishing tray.

I'm proud of it. I want to show it off. I want to put it up on one of my walls. I hold it up in every possible location and it doesn't look right anywhere. I stop. I listen. Maybe this piece is meant for somebody else?

My friend Debi who gave me the feathers sees it. She falls into the piece—figuratively, not literally. It takes her. I give it to her. I let go.

Decision by decision, I see how my path is unfolding organically. In spite of all the uncertainty surrounding my life's purpose, career, finances, relationships—and all those other uncertainties which make one's parents wish you had only listened to them and taken that civil service position years ago, so now you wouldn't have to worry—this path is leading me somewhere. It is up to me to listen and follow. Will someone please hand me my trail mix? I am stepping into the present moment.

Keep company with the silence of your soul.

~~~ Steps to Happiness NOW! ~~~

1) If you have a problem, eat at a chinese restaurant

Imagine shrinking your biggest problem into a Chinese food take-out box. Sometimes I imagine shrinking ex-lovers into the box. I pretend they're munchkin-sized and have little itsy bitsy voices. Even when they scream, "Help. Let me out of here," I can go about my day with greater focus and ease, knowing that although I still need to deal with the situation, it's no longer bigger than I am.

2) **Realize God moonlights as a sanitation engineer**

When problems persist, they rot. Someone's got to take out the garbage. Sometimes, God, Higher Power, or whatever you might want to call it, intervenes on our behalf, catalyzing us to let go of what we no longer need—whether we want to or not. This intervention is often perceived as a crisis, however the intent is always to teach us something we need to learn.

3) **Breathe through your nose and hang on by your toes**

Have you ever noticed when you're in the midst of one major life crisis, another one usually joins it? Then another one and another one, until you've got crises multiplying faster than rabbits? At some point you may feel so overwhelmed you begin to doubt the existence of God, or that if there is a God, this God really cares about you. Have faith.

4) **Sometimes, you have to give time, time (courtesy of my friend, Kristan Leatherman)**

During tough times you may feel like you're not going to make it. If you feel like you're dying inside or it gets so bad you feel like exiting the planet, hold on. A part of you *is* dying—that's the good news. Some old part of yourself is leaving so that a new, more empowered and happier part can emerge.

Three Pieces of Advice and More about Couches

"Life's too short. Have *fun*. Then make money."
—Mom

"Do whatever in your life makes you happy, but *make sure* it makes you happy."—Dad

"When in doubt, get the hell out."—My brother, Ted

It's Story Time...

How my family views me:

My mother looks on the positive side of life. "My daughter's not unemployed," she proudly says. "She's a writer."

My father thinks everything I do is "nice." If I play him a new piece of music I've just created, his response is always, "That's nice, honey." I play many instruments. My father is tone-deaf. He once told me everything sounds like the "Star-Spangled Banner" to him. Imagine what a real treat that must be. I think what he really wishes for me is that I meet a "nice" Jewish boy, who has a "nice" job and a "nice" retirement plan.

Like I said before, my brother, Ted, tells me outright, "Your friends are a bunch of New Age Flakes. None of them works a full-time job and they're all poor." Judge and jury, signed, sealed, delivered. If I was making a six or more figure income in the pursuit of my dreams, would that remove me from the category of flakism?

I can hear my brother's voice echoing in my brain, "Randy, you need to get off the couch and find a job in the real world."

Technically speaking, I'm not a New Age Flake because I don't own a couch. It's not that I don't want a couch, it's just that I have no room for one. Besides, I have early childhood couch memories.

When I was little, my parents had a couch with dark, ugly vertical stripes of black, blue, and gray. In the Seventies, it was covered with an off-white Naugahyde, which wasn't much of an improvement. Over the forty years of its existence, the legs gave out one at a time. Each time this happened, my mother propped up the broken end with my father's big old geology textbooks from the Forties. Thereafter she always referred to it as the "the seat of knowledge," thereby replacing the toilet as the holder of that auspicious honor.

You know what I've noticed about couches anyway? Whenever I've been at the home of a friend who has one, if the floor is carpeted, that's where we sit. And that expensive piece of furniture intended to be sat upon is used as a backrest to support us in holding up our nonmatching cups of tea.

If a coffee table runs interference, then we have even less space in the room, because we still don't sit on the couch. We just sit on the carpet on the other side of the coffee table, with less space for our legs and nothing to support our backs.

Couches are great for watching TV. None of us watches TV anymore. However, it feels good to stretch out on a couch and curl up with a good book. So they do serve a purpose after all.

Ultimately it doesn't matter whether others think my friends are flakes or whether I own a couch or not. Only I get to decide what is right for me—I choose my friends and I choose my furniture. The bottom line is no matter where I sit, the comfiest place for me to be is always at the center of a loving heart.

Furnish your home with love.

~~~Steps to Happiness NOW!~~~

5) Take my advice—don't take my advice

A teenager said to his mom, "Get off my case." And the mom replied, "I'm not on your case. If I was, I'd solve it." This kid was lucky. He got to figure his life out himself. Advice can hinder us from knowing our truth, because it's somebody else's truth, not ours. Stay away from giving or receiving advice unless it's requested. Each of us needs to be able to make our own decisions and find our own way.

6) Don't make someone else's story your own

If you sincerely want to do something, don't let anyone else's story stop you from creating what you want. Other people's lessons are not yours. When I hear someone whose story sounds somewhat similar to mine, I have to remind myself my situation is different because I am me, and she is her. My story is my story, and his is his.

7) Take back your life

If we are unhappy, there is often a large part of ourselves we are giving away. Whether we're consciously aware of it or not, we're no longer being true to ourselves. When we're not being true to ourselves, we've made an internal compromise; we're creating someone else's dream at the expense of our own.

8) Celebrate a new holiday—daughter's and son's day

Many parents have disowned their kids because they disapprove of their value system or lifestyle. To close a heart from a child wounds everybody concerned. You don't have to like 'em, but it helps if you love 'em—even if your child has tattoos, breeds snakes, and wears a nipple ring. They'll find their own way. Love them with all your heart. That's all they've ever needed—no matter what.

The New Age Flake Test

It's Story Time...

Do you believe in the afterlife more than you believe in your current life? Have you ever been known to chant in weird languages or contort your body into strange postures for the sake of inner peace and relaxation?

I've attended not one, but two, cow dung-burning ceremonies for inner purification. I've eaten ginseng energy bars while reading Deepak's latest book. I have no interest in channel-surfing through sports programs on TV—I channel angels instead.

Oh, my God! What if my brother is right? Am I a New Age Flake after all?

New Age used to be such a cool term. Look at what it says about the New Age in my 1992 Fictionary Dictionary: "New Age:" <Noun> *A time of peace. An uplifted state of consciousness where each person is nurtured to fulfill his or her greatest dream and reach his or her highest potential.*

And look at what it said about the term New Age Flake: <Noun> *A blend of fifteen wheat-free, corn-free, soy-free grains topped with dehydrated blueberries, and flavored with real maple syrup.*

Obviously, over time that meaning has changed. Now look at what it says in the updated version of my Fictionary Dictionary: "New Age Flake:" <Noun> *One who sits upon the couch, watching TV talk shows while waiting for God to produce his or her needed miracle.*

Has the New Age only produced a generation of flakes? The New Age couldn't have been ALL that bad, could it? Every path has its pearls of wisdom. Here's what I have learned from the New Age:

A) We must discover our life's purpose and live our dreams.

In other words, we must let go of that which provides our paycheck or other current sense of security and bungee jump into the void while believing a Loving Presence will catch us before we go splat on the pavement. As we enter into the unknown and stretch beyond our comfort zone, it is only natural that all of our fears will rise to the surface. When we feel like we re about to go splat on the pavement, it is often the case that we are actually being taught how to learn to live in faith and trust that we will always be taken care of.

B) We can manifest everything we desire.

In other words, we are all capable of manifesting anything because we realize our universe is infinitely abundant. If I now have a beautiful new car that my parents bought me, does it still count as an act of manifestation? You bet it does. There are many ways that the Universe can accommodate our wishes, from the most obvious, to the most mystical and magical of unforeseen circumstances.

C) We create our own reality.

In other words, we are responsible for how we deal with every crappy thing that happens to us. I'm not sure we create everything that happens to us, but I do know we can create how we *choose to react* to whatever happens to us.

D) **Judging ourselves or others is a no-no.**
In other words, if you judge yourself or another, don't judge yourself for being judgmental. Each of us needs to learn or accomplish something different in this life. My lessons aren't the same as yours. And everyone has her own sense of right timing. How long is your fuse before you lose patience or compassion with yourself or others?

E) **We deserve to live a life of happiness and prosperity.**
Unfortunately, this has often been misinterpreted as, "I want. I want. I want. Gimme. Gimme. Me. Me. Me." What it really means is that happiness and properity are every person's birthright. In addition, if our sense of deserving is colored by a tone of self-righteousness, we cannot attract happiness or prosperity to ourselves. However, if our sense of deserving contains no threads of resentment, it can positively impact our ability to create happiness and prosperity.

So I ask you, "What's wrong with the New Age? It's taught us some pretty valuable lessons, hasn't it? Maybe there's nothing wrong with being a New Age Flake. I know I'd personally feel a lot better if I knew I was surrounded by others who were just like me. Would you join me so I don't feel so alone?

To see if you qualify, answer the following statements with "True," "False," or "Comic attempt on the part of the author to elicit participation from the reader."

THE NEW AGE FLAKE TEST
(True or False)

LIFE'S PURPOSE

A. I know what my highest calling is.
B. I know what I want, who I am, and where I'm headed.
C. I am being true to my highest calling.
D. My highest calling is the sixty-four dollar phone call I made to Aunt Martha in Topeka last Tuesday morning.

WILLINGNESS TO RISK

A. I am willing to cling desperately to a job, relationship, or situation I know is wrong for me.
B. I am willing to let go of the security of a relationship or job if I know it is not my true heart's desire.
C. I am willing to risk everything to create the life I want.
D. I am willing to risk a pocketful of crumbs to create the life I want.
E. I am willing to watch someone else risk everything to create the life he wants, and then hit him up for a loan to create the life I want.

SELF-RESPONSIBILITY

A. I am willing to take responsibility for everything that happens to me.
B. I am willing to take responsibility for everything that happens to me except for the things I don't want to take responsibility for.
C. All my problems are someone else's fault.
D. All my problems are because of some other person/event/situation—it's still not my fault.

E. It's God's fault.
F. I'm fine. Everyone else is the problem.
G. Problems? What problems?

JUDGMENT

A. I don't care if other people think I'm weird.
B. It's okay if I act weird. However, it is not okay if other people act weird.

QUALITY OF LIFE

A. If I had my perfect job or relationship, I would be happy.
B. If I had my perfect job or relationship, I would know it.
C. I am living the life I want. Life is great! And I'm happy, happy, happy!
(If true, just wait three months—things change…)

We create our reaction to every given circumstance.

Steps to Happiness NOW!

9) Notice when the judges are judging, but don't let their judgments become law

Most of us have a panel of judges in our heads or in our lives. Judge Mom says, "You should…." Judge Dad says, "That's stupid." Your dear friend who wants to protect you from being hurt says, "I don't think it'll work." Judge Sibling says, "You're one flake short of a Cheerio." Judge Spouse says, "Please stop. You're embarrassing me." And some teacher's voice from the third grade is telling you, "You're doing it all wrong."

10) **Censor the censor within**

How many times have *you* stopped yourself from doing or saying something because you're afraid of what others might think? Or because you're afraid you can't do something perfectly the first time you try? Or because you know someone who can do it much better than you? Quit comparing yourself to others.

11) **Your ingredients are unique and so are you**

Pretend you've made a salad for a potluck. Other people might make salads too, and it's guaranteed they're not identical. You have your gift to bring to the table and they have theirs. People will pick and choose what they like. Nobody's right or wrong, better than or worse than. It's just a matter of individual taste.

12) **Empty the courtroom**

Notice who cheers you on, even if you start with only one person—yourself. Gradually replace the courtroom in your head with your cheering section. The longer you persevere, and the more you believe in yourself, the more others will too.

Randy's Dish Theory of Personality Discernment

It's Story Time...

The world is made up of only two kinds of people—those who own matching dishes and those who don't. I am here to tell you that people with matching dishes have different value systems and lifestyles than people whose dishes don't match.

The people who are most likely to call others "flakes" have matching dishes. People with matching dishware value the world of appearances. They tend to own their homes instead of rent. They usually have regular day jobs and families with kids that fight. They also entertain clients, and barbecue salmon outdoors on their gas grills every summer.

On the other hand, people whose dishes don't match value individuality. They tend to be creative types like artists or writers. They are all somewhat eccentric and have a motley assortment of friends, none of whom would mind sleeping on a couch or futon. Those with nonmatching dishware most likely do not own their own homes. They are definitely not married, although they might be single parents. More likely, they are parenting their boyfriend's eight-year-old from his previous marriage. Or even more likely, they are parenting their boyfriends.

What do people with nonmatching dishes do when they get angry? Sulk, then talk in "I" statements to work things out.

What do people with service for twelve do when they get really angry? They throw their dishes. Often unbeknownst to them at a conscious level, smashing their dishes represents an act of rebellion toward their entire value system. The next afternoon, though, they run to Macy's to buy a whole new set.

If I opened your kitchen cabinet, what would I find? A shelf of one-of-a-kind mugs? Perhaps some with chips around their rims? Or plates from various garage sales?

Or would I find service for twelve? Perhaps a pre-World War II set of fine Nippon stored in its very own china cabinet?

Now, if you have some of each, one of three options is possible. If your nonmatching dishware outnumbers your matching set, you are attempting in your own unique way to conform to society's standards. In reality though, you're not there.

On the other hand, if you own some pieces of nonmatching items but mostly have matching dishware, you are desiring to step out on a limb, but not as far as Shirley MacLaine would.

The third possibility is, you have an equal number of nonmatching and matching dishes. In this case, you are a multiple personality who needs to seek out a therapist who specializes in dishware.

An important disclaimer: If you have matching dishes because you inherited them, you may still have the underlying personality of one whose dishes don't match.

Since it is not your astrological sign but your dishware that ultimately determines your fate, I suggest you really think twice about the kinds of dishes you choose to keep. Do your dishes reflect "the real you?" You be the judge.

Dish up a great life for yourself!

13) Take down the dart board

I don't really want to be thought of as a New Age Flake. I bet you don't like being called names either. We can use our words to help or we can use our words to hurt. With the first word that feels hurtful, walls go up. Then with each subsequent hurtful word or interaction, more walls go up. Anger builds and pretty soon the verbal darts are flying back and forth through the air. Be conscious of your words.

14) When you speak, build bridges instead of barriers

What if our goal was to create a bridge to every person we encountered? So if something hurtful gets said, we'd want to immediately restore comfort and safety to that interaction and to our relationship with that person. How would that be?

15) Recognize the intention behind the words

Notice if you are carrying any hurts from the recent or distant past. Did someone intentionally hurt you (if so, can you remove him or her from your life or put greater limits on the amount of contact you have)? Or did this person just say something that felt hurtful in the moment? Each time you speak up about a hurt, and the sooner you do, the better you'll feel, as each situation is brought to resolution.

16) **Put more kindness and love into the world**

Think before you speak. Are your words loving and kind? Or are you intentionally zinging the other person? You know the intent behind your words. Is your goal to create a bridge or to cause more hurt because you feel hurt?

And You Call Yourself an Adult?

It's Story Time...

Who said that? I did not call myself an adult. I am forty years old. I have one gray hair. Okay, maybe three. I also wear bifocals and I'm losing my eggs. However, I am not an adult!

The avant-garde rock singer, Laurie Anderson, said in the *Village Voice* that when she turned forty she couldn't decide whether that meant she felt more like four ten-year-olds or ten four-year-olds.

Laurie Anderson doesn't feel like an adult either. If she doesn't have to, then I don't have to. Whoops, I forgot I can make that decision for myself. I don't have to listen to anyone else. I'm an adult. OOPS. I didn't mean to say that. I take it back.

For years, all of my friends have worked to get in touch with their inner child. I've always been in touch with my inner child. The challenge for me has been to get in touch with my inner adult.

My first idea of what an adult was came when I was a little girl and saw my mother put on earrings because she was going out. Therefore, putting on earrings made an adult. When I was in high school I got my ears pierced.

I was really excited about my first venture into the world of adulthood. Unbeknownst to me until it was too late, I was also allergic to gold, and the earrings started to pull through the bottom of my earlobes. I couldn't wear them. That proved it. I could never officially become an adult.

That's okay because adults don't know how to have fun. Adults make themselves black-and-blue with self-criticism. Adults hold back out of fear of what others think, or because they're comparing themselves to someone else who they think is better.

~~~You Can't Squash an Eepster~~~

I was just reading a page or two from a famous author's book. She's an adult. She was talking about how, when she first started writing, she was witty and clever and touched people's hearts; and now that she's more experienced, she makes her characters less witty and more real.

I interpreted this to mean that my writing, which is witty and clever and heart-touching (it is, isn't it?) wasn't good enough. Nasty, bad critic of self has stepped in. SQUASH. Some mean old adult in my head is telling me I can't do it. I haven't written a word for four days. Nothing is coming through. The door is slammed shut.

Help! I've got to get the critical adult out of my head or start taking in laundry. I don't own a washing machine. This narrows my choices. This means I've got to get the critic out of my head, quick!

I know who I need. I need the Eepster!

Once upon a time, long ago, I was in a session with a therapist who was helping me to find the smallest of the inner children in my vast collection.

I was finally able to identify her. She was so tiny, all she could do was huddle in a corner and say, "eep." She spoke in a little, mousy voice, and no one heard her or paid any attention to her.

I worked on getting the little Eepster to express herself more. I eeped in my car crossing the Golden Gate Bridge. I bought her a gorgeous Celtic harp and called it Eep's Harp. I eeped to my bird, Sweet Pea, in response to his sweet songs. Eventually I added a flapping motion with my arms when I'd eep to him, and this behavior has stuck with me.

Over the years, I've felt safer and safer to let the Eepster express more and more. Now I eep and flap. And sometimes I do these things in public. Today the Eepster has no trouble eeping in a crowd, sometimes accompanied by flapping and a happy tongue sticking out, if she's extremely excited about something.

You might think eeping and flapping are strange behaviors or that I am weird or immature. Am not! Am not!

Instead of judging me right now, try using the word, "different," as in "Gee, she has a different way of expressing herself." Then leave it at that. To notice without judging is a powerful personal position to take.

The therapist liked the Eepster a lot when she first met her. She asked if she could share the Eepster story with other clients. I was delighted. She encouraged them to express their teeny-tiniest selves with an "eep." Now there are fulfilled women happily "eeping" all over the Bay Area. I swear to you this is true.

It never hurts to put a little magic out in the world, and this is the Eepster's realm. Eepsters don't worry about other people's reactions. An Eepster is free to express herself in any way that makes her happy.

When I feel the energy of the Eepster, I can write without fear of judgment or criticism. I can laugh at myself more. Everything is good enough for the Eepster, because the Eepster exists to express pure joy—the joy of being alive. And life is more fun with an Eepster around.

I don't want to be one of those boring grown-ups who's afraid to take a chance or make a mistake or be silly or has forgotten how to laugh. I want to play with people and touch the hearts of those I come in contact with.

So there, famous writer person who says "I'm not good enough" in my head. Adios. Bye-bye. Ciao. Pasta Luigi. You're history, yesterday's news, not tomorrow's headlines. You can't squash an Eepster! She's back in control!

Don't get me wrong, I can be responsible and do adultlike things with adultlike proficiency, but with the Eepster, I'm happier and more willing to risk.

~ How to Tell If You're an Eepster ~

Adults don't mount bean pots on stands because they sound good when you hit them. Eepsters do. Adults don't march through their house chanting, "House Parade, I'm on house parade." Eepsters do. Adults don't drum in the Laundromat. Eepsters do and Eepsters will.

Adults say, "No, you can't" to others, or "No, I can't," to themselves. When kids are playing, they don't stop themselves in midsentence to think whether they can be something or not. They just go for it. A kid at play might say, "I'm Babaroo, king of the Universe," and believe it.

If Babaroo is lucky, his parents will say, "Yeah, you're Babaroo, king of the Universe." However, other adults would say, "No, you're Joshua Greenfield who needs to come in and do your homework, right now!" What a bummer. What joy we miss by conforming to someone else's version of reality.

Adults don't do a thing just because it makes them happy. Eepsters do. Adults need to accomplish something. Adults do things to get something done. That's how they know they're adults.

The only reason eepsters do a thing is because it makes them happy. Since I was a little kid, I've always wanted to be a drummer. And for years, I've always known I was a great drummer. It took me until my thirties before I could realize this dream. But I did. And I am a great drummer. In fact, I'm one of the best drummers in the world.

I love to drum. Drumming fills me with a joy I can't describe. It is the joy of an Eepster. It is that joy, that love that comes through, that makes me the greatest drummer in the world. No one can touch that. No one can criticize that.

And it doesn't preclude you from being the greatest drummer in the world either, if that's what you want. Eepsters have no need to hoard joy and greatness. In the Eepster's world, anyone can be the greatest at anything.

I am often asked if I play in a band. That's not where it's at for me. I have no need to perform. And in fact, performing terrifies me. I drum because I love to and for no other reason. I sit and drum by myself for hours. It gives me joy, and that is enough.

Recently I met a drummer with twenty more years of experience than I have. I could feel him judging my playing, and I knew I could never be great in his eyes. Eepsters have no use for judges, so I didn't pursue a friendship with him.

I don't surround myself with people who are critical of me. Instead, I surround myself with people who say, "Wow, you're a great drummer! You have so much joy when you play. Can we play together?" This makes an Eepster very happy.

I find the people who make the best friends for me are the ones who support me in my greatness. The ones I weed out are the ones who don't think I am great, or even could be, or who don't hold the highest vision for me.

For example, as I was writing this book, a friend came over and told me how the market was flooded with books and even if I got it published, the likelihood of it being a bestseller was low.

I listened to his lack of enthusiasm and thought, "This is someone who doesn't hold the highest vision for me because he probably doesn't hold the highest vision for himself." I spoke with him about his lack of positive response, to which he replied, "I was just playing the devil's advocate. I really do like the book."

Although he expressed that he really did feel positively about the book, I knew this was not the kind of spark that would keep my fire fueled. So I decided to only share my thoughts with the people who held me and my book in the brightest possible light.

When I spoke with another friend about his comments, she said, "Don't listen to that baloney. Your book is great. Keep going. Hit those keys." That's a friend who believes in the Eepster.

There, that feels much better. Whose voice do I want to listen to anyway? Adults squash the life out of me. Fellow Eepsters support me in doing what I love to do just because I love to do it.

I like being an Eepster. I'm being the best Eepster I can be. I can play in the adult world. But for me, it's only play. Thank God, the Eepster has returned.

It's your life. Do it the way you want to. The Eepster dares you!

17) Put your grown-up-self down for a nap and let your child-self come out and play

Enjoying oneself—let's call it "play"—is vital to being happy. Observe children at play. Unless they are fighting, they are having fun. That's the whole purpose of play. If you check the rulebook for grown-ups, I bet you won't find any rule that says at a certain age you have to give up playing.

18) If it's fun, it's play

When you play, it's important to do something not goal-oriented. Do it just because it is fun. Do it because it is something you love to do. When you were a kid, do you remember looking forward to recess? Start scheduling play into your daily appointment book. Having fun deserves your time and attention as much as working and making money.

19) Turn off the TV (Is she serious?)

The television not only baby-sits children, it baby-sits adults as well. Upon taking a walk in my neighborhood one evening, the glow of a TV set was visible from every house. If I multiply my neighborhood by the millions of neighborhoods around the country, that's a lot of people being baby-sat, and being lulled away from fulfilling forms of creativity. If you can't imagine living without TV, try unplugging it for just a month as an experiment. See what happens. (Okay, you can still tape your favorite shows!)

20) Spend quality time with good friends instead of good machines

In addition to the TV set, people now spend their lives in front of computer screens rather than with friends. Friends contribute greatly to our feelings of happiness. Our friends know our ups and downs and all-arounds and still like us. Remember, machines wear out faster than friends do, unless you keep on neglecting them.

SECTION 2

NAVIGATING THE RAPIDS

Managing Life's Challenges with Grace

- Some of our garbage floats in front of our eyes while other parts of it have sunken to the bottom of our "inner see." It is only through our willingness to plumb these depths and deal with the tough stuff that we can bring about a shift in the way we perceive ourselves, each other, and the world.

- In this section, we'll learn "Crisis First Aid"—techniques for dealing with situations that feel overwhelming or impossible.

- We'll explore ways to deal with loss, death and grief, mis-communication in relationships, bosses from hell, old cars that go into cardiac arrest in the middle of a freeway, and all those things that make us feel like the deck of Life is stacked against us.

If Time Doesn't Exist, Then No One Ever Leaves

It's Story Time...

When I was a little girl, I heard that people with long earlobes lived longer than people with short earlobes. Go to the mirror. Check your earlobes.

Eat dinner with your friends. Make soup that night, maybe a nice chicken vegetable soup, or minestrone. It could be canned, but it'll taste better if it's homemade. If you're a lousy cook, then buy some Ramen noodles and just heat and serve. It doesn't matter. Make what you want.

Give your friends rubber bands and tell them to pull their hair behind their ears so it doesn't fall in the soup. When they pull their hair back, check their earlobes. Earlobes that are long because of heavy earrings don't count. It's a great plan. They'll never suspect a thing.

As a little girl, I remember checking to see if my grandma Ida had long earlobes and she did. (She wasn't wearing heavy earrings either). This made me very happy because I wanted her to live for a long time. And she has. She is almost 98 years old. She has even outlived the Energizer Bunny. The earlobe theory is true. When I was about four years old, I remember saying to her, "I love you so much, there are no numbers." Either I loved her a whole lot or I just didn't know how to count yet. I guess the former is true, because I still feel that way about her, and maybe the latter is true too, because I never was good at math.

I've always had this special relationship with my grandmother. My grandma loves and accepts me exactly as I am. She has never ever said one unkind word to me, not even accidentally. She has never shamed or embarrassed me. She loves me in a way I don't experience anywhere else in my life. She loves me without limits, expectations, or conditions.

My grandma's got this great, thicker than cream cheese, Hungarian Yiddish accent. It is actually because of this accent that my name is Randy. My mom wanted to name me "Wendy," but she knew that my grandmother would pronounce that "Vendy." My mother didn't want me to be a "Vendy." So I became a "Randalah" instead.

And I love being a Randalah. My grandmother has always called me Randalah, my shaynila maidalah (Randy, my Shining Maiden). (You can't call me that, only she can.) No matter how old I am, I will always be my grandma's shaynila maidalah.

My grandma is deeply connected to the world of Spirit. She has a faith in God that I find hard to fathom sometimes. She tells me, "Randalah, God will never disappoint you. You will be healthy and happy and safe and prosperous. Just smile. Don't worry. If I could give you one gift, it would be the gift not to worry."

I don't understand how someone who lost her mother and most of her family in the Holocaust can still have faith and believe in God. However, she does. Her faith is very strong. "The plane needs a pilot, the ship needs a captain, and we need God," she says.

For years I've worried about her dying, and like the four-year-old still so connected to her, I hope that magically it won't happen.

Some years ago, we thought she was getting ready. She rejected all gifts, stopped watching TV, and gave away her clothing. She seemed to be getting weaker and weaker, was losing her eyesight, and was growing more and more despondent. Then her thinking got fuzzy.

She was taken from the nursing home and put into a hospital, at which point she refused to swallow any more medications. She just clamped her mouth shut and refused—and she got well. Her thinking became clear. Her hearing improved. She returned to the nursing home. It turned out she was being overmedicated.

One night shortly after that, she had a dream in which her mother came to her. She'd always been very close to her mother, Rose. She dreamt her mother came to her and removed splinters from her eyes.

When she woke up in the morning, her sight had been restored. She was able to read large-print books again. She turned her TV back on and caught up with the news of the world. It was such a remarkable turnaround.

One day she said to my mother. "You know, Harriet, I was praying to die, and look, now I'm living."

And my mother said to her, "Perhaps you were praying for the wrong thing."

Two years later we again thought she was going to die, so I went back East to be with her. I sat down next to the bed, reached through the railing and took her frail hand in mine. All the love of her heart poured through her eyes as she said to me, "Randalah, mamalah shayna, I love you so much there are no numbers. You have a special place in my heart which is just for you. I will always love you no matter what."

When my grandma tells me how much she loves me, I just let the tears stream down my face. This is real love. This is unconditional love. My grandma knows all my secrets and she *still* loves me.

(Secrets? What secrets? Who said I have secrets?)

My grandma has always said she wanted to live to see me get married. I was afraid to tell her I had spent the last ten years in and out of relationships with people of my own gender. I didn't know if she would judge me or stop loving me, and besides, my mother said that my grandma had a weak heart and this would kill her.

Now this is a predicament. I want to live in my truth and I wanted to tell her, but would you kill your grandma? I'm no grandma-killer.

Well, eventually my mother took it upon herself to tell her. Recalling other family members, my grandmother's matter of fact response was, "You know, I think Xaviera and Ulysses (not their real names) are, too." That was it. No big dramatics. No heart attack. And I am still deeply loved regardless of whom I love, how I love, or whom I'm with or not with.

Another three years have gone by. Now my grandma is completely deaf. She doesn't want to eat anymore. She wants to leave.

If I believe what I've heard and read, once we die, turn in our ticker, or boogie-woogie into a bodiless reality, we are no longer bound by the constraints of time. Well, if there's no such thing as time, then we can be here now, there then, in the future, in the past, or wherever we like. If we can be anywhere at any time, it makes sense to me that there's no more separation—hence, no one ever leaves.

If no one ever leaves, all the therapists will go out of business because everyone's abandonment issues will be solved once and for all. Just think of it. Your partner just left you, and you don't want to let go. Anyway, here's what you can do. Step off the time continuum. Hop back to last year or hang out in 1974. Remember a year you really liked and go there, or jump forward to your birthday in 2012 and throw yourself a party.

No one ever leaves—what a concept. Use this concept topically, and for deeper wounds, apply as often as necessary. Of course, if you are in a relationship from hell and you never want to see that person ever again, then just never mind about this idea altogether.

However, it works for me. I hate good-byes. I hate leaving. I hate being left. I don't want her to go.

And she is ready to leave.

Others say to me, "Well, she's lived a long life," as if that makes her dying acceptable. This still doesn't cut it for me. I don't care how old she is, she's still my grandma, and I don't want her to die. That's it, plain and simple.

I guess what I want to say is, "When it's your time, Grandma, happy journeys to a land that is bright and beautiful. May the loving angels always be by your side. I am happy you will get to see Grandpa, your mom, and your family. I will always think about you, miss you, and pray for you. You have been the best grandma in the world and there will never be enough numbers to say how much I love you. Thank you for all you have given to me. I know all is well and that you are a bright and shining star in the Universe. I love you forever."

Love, Randy

To love is to pray for someone else's highest good, even if it means you have to let her go.

~~~ Steps to Happiness NOW! ~~~

21) Know what really matters

Fancy cars are pieces of metal that eventually rust. Fancy houses are pieces of wood (or whatever) that eventually rot. Unconditional love is rustproof and termite-proof. It withstands all the tests of time.

22) If a miracle landed in your lap, would you notice it?

To be loved unconditionally is a miracle. It is one of the greatest gifts we can experience. Sometimes a special being enters our lives who gives us that kind of love. If you are blessed with such a person, acknowledge he is a miracle in your life and give great thanks for his presence.

23) Unconditional love helps everyone breathe easier

Unconditional love is the only kind of love never withheld for any reason. It allows you the freedom to discover your own answers, and to make your own mistakes if need be, while always wanting the best for you. Unconditional love accepts each being exactly as she is, regardless of personal choice or lifestyle.

24) Open your heart, your love is needed

Unconditional love demands nothing and gives everything. It does not judge and it does not condemn. Unconditional love is a balm for the heart. (Not a bomb, a balm.) It often elicits joyous tears, because this kind of love is the strongest healing agent in the Universe. Start giving your love away and watch how your supply increases.

A Most Magnificent Journey

IT'S STORY TIME...

The phone rang. It was my mom. My grandmother Ida had stopped eating. I knew what this meant. My grandma was dying.

I was afraid. I was afraid of death. I was afraid to be with her when she died. I was afraid of all the grief I was going to feel. And I was afraid of everyone else's pain, too.

I knew I could stay in California and let her die without me, but I couldn't do that. As frightened as I was, I wanted to hold her hand and be there for her.

It was time to mobilize. Flights into Connecticut cost $1400. The cheapest flight I could find was to Boston. Hartford was where I needed to go. I couldn't afford it.

Night came. I hurried to a support group that assisted people with loved ones with a chronic illness or a life-threatening condition. The people in the group were warm and supportive. I felt cared about and comforted. One woman, her eyes also moistened with tears, shared how close she was with her grandmother who had died, and that what she missed most was being able to touch her.

Another woman, thirty years old, who had just lost her fiancé and had barely been able to eat or sleep for the entire week, said to me, "If you want, when I get home tonight I'll call some airlines and see what I can find." She really meant it.

After the group ended, she took my phone number and told me she would call a few hours later with the results.

Her willingness to help reminded me I was not alone. I made a mental note that I had help and support as long as I was willing to let it in. I could have just as easily said to her, "No, that's okay, I'll figure it out," and let her offer go. But I didn't. I accepted her help.

Later on she told me, "Thank you so much for letting me help. If I couldn't have, I would have felt tortured. I needed to be able to give, because it's the only thing which makes me feel life is worth living right now."

I was reminded that when I was willing to accept help, it allowed another the opportunity to give. And the opportunity to give was as great a gift to the giver as the outcome was to the receiver.

She phoned at 11:30 that night, with the news she couldn't find a better rate. However, she gave me an excellent idea—rent a laptop computer, so while I was away I could continue to work on my book. However long I stayed in Connecticut, this would help me to maintain a somewhat normal routine.

The next morning I was speaking with my friend Aileen, a very nurturing and maternal force in my life as well as a psychic. Aileen told me my grandma was hanging on because my mother and I would not let her go. She encouraged me to consciously send messages to my grandma that it was okay for her to go and that she had my blessing.

Instinctively, I knew Aileen was right. But how could I do this? I didn't want my grandma to die. I didn't want to let her go. Then I thought of how my grandma was suffering. I started forming the words in my mind. "Grandma, it's okay. I love you. You're the best grandma in the world and it's okay for you to go." I couldn't bring myself to say them out loud, so I said the words over and over in my mind, getting used to the idea.

I called the travel agent and arranged the flight to Boston, which was leaving at one in the morning from San Francisco. Next I rented a laptop. Then discovering I had no clean clothes, I scurried over to the Laundromat.

As I was carting in my clothes, a man was working on his van right out in front. The logo on the side of the van made me realize he was the boyfriend of a woman I knew. "Aren't you Anne's friend?" He answered, "Yes."

We talked for a few seconds and I told him my grandma was dying. He offered to say a prayer for all of us when he did his daily meditation, and also said if there was anything he could do, I should let him know.

An hour later, tears flowing, I went back to pick up my laundry. The man was still by his van and I said to him, "I'm not doing so well right now." This man, who I'd just met and was virtually a total stranger to me, stopped what he was doing, put his arms around me, and held me. Then he invited me to sit down in his shop next door and talk.

Once more, I noticed how people—even people I barely knew, were willing to help if I let them.

We talked for a bit and, feeling calmer, I left to make phone calls. My friends would be concerned and I wanted to let them know what was happening.

First I called Elizabeth. As I told her my grandma was dying, immediately the tears were back. I began to feel frantic and upset. Elizabeth listened attentively as I talked and cried. She told me how difficult it had been for her to lose her grandpa the previous year.

Elizabeth was also going through something challenging. After sharing some of my grief and sadness, I was able to get quiet and give her my full attention. When she was through, I told her how surprised I was that I could switch gears so quickly, to get out of my emotional state and be totally present for her.

Elizabeth had a keen observation—"When you were crying and needing support, more of your 'inner child' was activated. When you were listening and giving support, you switched to your adult self." She pointed out how easily I could switch back and forth between the two.

Elizabeth was right. The child part of me was scared of death, wanted comfort and care, and was afraid of everything that was happening. The adult part of me could cope, handle details, and support others. If I wanted, I could feel like a child, needing comfort and support, or I could feel my adult-self and assist where needed. I could choose. I could activate one or the other. I decided to keep my inner adult very present through this experience.

Next, I needed to make arrangements to get to the bus for the airport. The bus station was ten minutes from my house. Although I could have called a cab, I wanted a friend to drive me because I was about to embark upon a difficult journey and I wanted someone to hug good-bye.

That night, I, who have a thousand friends, could not find a single person to bring me to the bus terminal. Some were too tired and others were too busy. No excuse was good enough for me that night. It felt as though no one was willing to go out of their way for me when I most needed their support.

Then I phoned my friend Carol just to tell her I was leaving in a few hours. Carol lived an hour and a half away. Although I hadn't even asked, Carol offered to drive me.

I was deeply touched. Here was someone who, without hesitation, was willing to go the extra mile, in fact many extra miles, for me.

I told Carol I didn't need her to come and get me. What I really needed all along was the offer. That degree of caring was what I needed. Feeling her love and support, I took a cab.

The journey to Connecticut would have been faster if I had taken the Wells Fargo pony wagon. At ten-thirty that night I took a taxi to the bus, then the bus to a plane, and the plane to another plane. Around noon the next day, I arrived in slushy, snowy, bitter-cold Boston and caught another cab to a bus headed to Hartford. Around 3:30 P.M., my father intercepted me at the Hartford bus station with the words, "Grandma is in bad shape. She might not make it through today."

We jumped in the car. "Floor it, Dad." It was an hour's trip to the nursing home and I wanted to get there as quickly as we could. I felt a sense of urgency. However, as we drove, I started to feel a different sensation. I felt we didn't have to hurry. I was still concerned and wanted to get there as quickly as possible, but I didn't feel frantic. I felt calm.

At 4:45 P.M., we arrived at the nursing home, and as my father pulled up to the entrance, I jumped out of the car and ran down the hallway to my grandma's unit. I burst into the room. My mom was there, a sweet smile on her face. My grandma Ida had died at 2:10 P.M., more than two hours earlier.

The previous year, I had interviewed Barbara Brennan, author of *Hands of Light* and *Light Emerging*. Barbara had told me if someone you love dies, try to stay open and not drown in your grief. The person who has died often has a great gift for you, and in order to receive it you must remain calm and open.

According to Barbara, if you were overwhelmed by grief, the gift couldn't be received and it was actually painful for the one who had died not to be able to give it. Barbara shared with me how she had received this gift, a beautiful flow of love, light, and wisdom, from her father when he passed over.

I was clear—I wanted to stay open to receive my grandmother's gift. My grandma had not been moved. She was still lying on the bed. Her body looked at peace. I felt happy for her. She was free. Now she could be with her mother and all who had passed over whom she loved. I, too, felt at peace. I stayed in my adult-self and my heart filled with love.

I recalled the woman in the group saying how much she missed being able to touch her grandmother. I leaned over and gently kissed my grandma's forehead. I was not afraid. I felt such a sweet love inside me. I reached through the covers and held her hand. I stroked her hair and her baby-soft skin until the memory was locked in my being.

Looking at my grandma's body, I realized I was looking at a shell. My grandma used to be in it. And now she was not there. The essence of my grandma was somewhere else, not in that shell.

In that moment, I lost my lifelong fear of death. All the years of fear—both of her dying and of anything related to death—melted away. I used to think when someone died, he was frozen in his body, like a movie actor pretending to be killed. That was not what I saw. My grandma simply was not in that shell any longer. She wasn't frozen in there. In fact, she wasn't in there at all!

I felt a profound sense of awe about the mystery of everything eternal. I remembered my grandmother's steady faith in God. And in this moment I also felt a deep faith in God and in the process of all living things.

My grandma was giving me great gifts.

I talked to her. It was strange talking to her body. However, I didn't know where else in the room to look. I figured if she was still in the room, which I assumed she was, she would understand I knew she wasn't in her body anymore. At the time it was a convenient place for me to focus my eyes. I told her I loved her forever and that she had done a great job at being the best grandma in the world.

The mortician was waiting in the hallway. He needed to take the body and had waited till the last minute so I could be there.

When we reached home, my mom started to lose it. She kept saying, "I can't believe my mother is dead. I just can't believe it." And I replied, "That's because she isn't. I don't think she's dead, I think she's more alive than before." I could feel it. I knew it. I could feel her love so strongly. My grandma was free.

I stayed in my adult self, giving support, comforting, talking, listening, sharing. Then my dad and I headed to a store to pick up some groceries. In the car I was hoping we would continue talking about our feelings. Instead, my father plunged into a conversation about brands of ice-cream he liked or disliked and his favorite basketball team.

I knew my father loved my grandmother. I couldn't fathom how he was just going on and on about all this trivial stuff as though nothing had happened. Then I realized everyone handles grief differently. Okay, Dad, let's talk about Fudgsicles.

The next day at the funeral, my four-year-old nephew Sam asked me if I was old. I told him I was just a little older than his daddy. He said, "No, that's not what I mean. Are you old and sick and going to die?" I comforted him. "No, Sam, I'm not."

A few times before the funeral started, I lost it too. My sister-in-law, Roxane, took my hand and squeezed my arm with her other hand. The support felt solid.

As I was feeling another wave of sadness, I leaned into my father. He put his arm around me and said, "I love you, honey." It felt so good to feel his love and support, too.

One of the kids started to grab my hand and swing. The playful kid energy distracted me from the feeling of helpless grief. It put a smile on my face. I realized there were many ways to heal.

The funeral was loving and intimate with my father conducting. Although not officially a rabbi, over the years my Dad, who is a biblical scholar, has often conducted services for the Jewish community in my parent's hometown. He read the appropriate prayers, spoke about the mother-in-law whom he treasured, and then invited the intimate assembly of aunts, uncles, cousins, and grandchildren to share as well.

As each of us took a turn talking, my Aunt Shirley, in her Joan Rivers' style of delivery, said, "My mother always called me and Harriet her two diamonds. She didn't need any other jewels. We were her gems. And when the kids used to tease me in school and call me fat, she'd tell me it was because they were all jealous."

My grandmother had given lots of love to everyone in her family through food. Chicken soup with matzo balls, chopped liver, potato latkes, Hungarian stuffed cabbage—no one could rival her expertise in the kitchen. She had been a phenomenal cook who had delighted in seeing the plump cheeks of someone well-fed.

We had a running joke in the family. If my grandmother told someone her face looked good, that meant by the rest of society's standards, she needed to go on a diet. I think she especially liked cooking for me because I was toothpick-thin when I was young.

Although she had lived in poverty for many years, she had always invited poorer people to eat with the family. She was one of those people who had a special kind of heart.

Everyone laughed at my aunt's story. My grandmother was definitely a "Yiddishe Mama" and that was what would be put on her tombstone: "Ida Fourman, Beloved Wife, Yiddishe Mama."

I told about the many gifts I had received from my grandmother, including the gift of unconditional love and the gift of faith. I spoke about my experience of being with her after she died, and how I lost my fear of death because of it. And I spoke about how I looked forward to communicating with her through my dreams or in whatever way she comes to me.

I wanted so much to ease the pain of the people gathered. I wanted everyone to know it was okay to die, that it was safe, and there was no need to fear death. Then I realized all I could do was share my own experience. Each person would integrate their experience and do exactly what they needed to do for themselves.

A week later, my sister-in-law overheard my four-year-old nephew Sam talking to his friends at preschool. Sam told them, "They packed my great-grandma in a Chanukah box as a gift to HaShem (God)."

Every year for Chanukah, my parents mailed a big box of toys to Alabama for their grandkids. Sam must have seen the Jewish star on the coffin and deduced that the casket was a "Chanukah box." I loved the part about great-grandma being a "gift to God." Sam got it right.

What a way to view the loss of a loved one—that they are being presented to God as a gift. It's one of the most brilliant and beautiful statements I've ever heard. The image of "packing great grandma" makes my heart smile and I'm sure my grandma has gotten a good laugh out of it too.

I thought about how I had worried about my grandmother dying for nearly thirty years. Back when she was in her early seventies, I remembered thinking she was getting old and I was terrified of losing her. I wondered who would be with me. Who would hold and comfort me when the dreaded event happened?

As the years went by, I thought about how each person I had been in relationship with would be the one to comfort me when she died. As each relationship ended, the hope of being held and comforted by that particular partner ended as well.

My grandmother's death and how I reacted to it never played out as I had feared or expected. I hadn't needed anyone to hold me. Surprisingly, I was the comforter who could be there for my mom and others.

I could not have predicted this outcome. It was what it was, and it happened the way it happened. Once again, I remembered my grandmother's words—"If I could give you one gift, it would be the gift not to worry. Things work out. Don't worry, mamaleh. It'll all work out."

I look forward to communicating with her. I picture her surrounded by love and I imagine God saying to her, "A job well done, Ida. You've done well." I picture her free, happy, and quite alive.

I learned there is no loss of love in the universe. The body may die, but never the soul. The essence of being, the spirit, goes on. And where there has once been love, there always will be love. Always.

Love goes on and on and on.

~~~ Steps to Happiness NOW! ~~~

25) Crunch the clock

Once while intensely grieving a loss, I was on the phone talking with my mother. Crying hysterically, I told her, "I don't know how I'm going to get through the day." I'll never forget her response. "Just get through the next hour, and if you can't do that, then just get through the next minute."

26) Notice beauty

Even when life feels unbearable, the birds still sing and the flowers still grow. Take every opportunity you can to notice the beauty surrounding you. It helps. Listen to the birds. Smell the beautiful scent of the flowers. Touch the smoothness of a stone.

27) Focus on that which is eternal

During a recent loss, my friend Mark said to me, "Now is the time to get in touch with that which is Eternal. Feel the sun on your face. Be with the mountains, the ocean, the trees." Walk in nature. It helps us to connect with that which goes on and on beyond our mortal preconceptions.

28) Be real. It gives others permission to do the same

Another time while grieving, I started talking to a man sitting next to me on a plane. Tears falling, I spilled my guts to this total stranger and guess what? Because of the depth of sharing, we developed a very special friendship. That was two years ago. Recently he told me that because of my honesty and vulnerability, he has always felt safe to express whatever he's feeling, too.

When Crisis Calls—
Don't Accept the Charges

It's Story Time...

Loss of any kind is painful. One of the things which has helped me to get through the numerous losses I've experienced (such as the death of loved ones, the death of pets, the end of relationships, and the end of jobs, to name a few) is a question my friend Debi asks herself whenever she has been in crisis:

"What's the most loving thing I can do for me right now?"

If you've ever experienced some heart-wrenching, gut-twisting, bubble-bursting slog through the depths of despair, gloomy end to a significant relationship—and you probably have because that's what happens to human beings—this question is one of the best tools to help you get through it all.

Here's how it worked for me a few days after Oshara, my long-time lover, (well, by my standards, a year and a half is a long time), had packed her bags and headed for another state:

> "Self, what's the most loving thing I can do for me right now?" I listen for the answer.
>
> "Cry."
>
> Ten minutes of wailing later—"Self, what's the most loving thing I can do for me right now?"

"Cry some more."

Okay, back at it.

A half hour later—"Self, what's the most loving thing I can do for me right now?"

"Do the dishes."

Okay, amidst the tears, the dishes are done.

After the dishes—"Self, what's the most loving thing I can do for me right now?"

"Take a walk."

"Self, what's the most loving thing I can do for me? I hate her. How could she do this to me?"

Self interrupts me—"No, that's not about you. Bring it back to you."

"Self," I argue, "I'm in pain. She hurt me. I'm angry at her."

Self answers back, "When you direct your energy outward and unload this blame on her for how bad you're feeling, you're focusing your attention on her and not on you. How can this help? You cannot change her or fix her. Instead, concentrate on doing the most loving thing that you could possibly do for yourself in this moment. Bring your attention back to your own loving heart and what would help *you* right now."

"Okay. Self, what's the most loving thing I can do for *me*?"

"Throw eggs—lots of 'em!"

With the passage of time, Oshara has become a dearly loved, close friend. Recently, she was in the midst of having a crappy day, so I asked her the question, "What's the most loving thing you can do for yourself right now?"

Her immediate response was, "Go shopping."

"In that case," I replied, "What's the most loving thing you can do for *me* today?"

Actually she already did a very loving thing for me this week. She surprised me with a printer for my computer so I could print out my book as I worked on it. What a gal! And we don't even sleep together anymore!

Remember this question—"What's the most loving thing I can do for me right now?" It comes in handy when life feels very fragile.

Commit to doing the most loving thing for yourself always.

~~~ Steps to Happiness NOW! ~~~

29) Sorrow digs the well and joy fills it

Years ago, I realized that the deeper I could go in my sorrow, the deeper my capacity for joy would be. I also learned that if I wasn't willing to feel the depths of pain, I would not be able to feel the heights of joy.

30) Crying turns us into butterflies

When life feels like it's closing in on us, we often experience a meltdown. Much like the caterpillar that liquefies inside the chrysalis before it becomes a butterfly, we too turn to liquid—our emotions turn to tears. And the more tears we cry, the more we can release what is no longer needed in order to complete our transformation into beautiful butterflies.

31) Surrender, Dorothy

Some people think melting down is a sign of weakness because one is made very vulnerable in the process. Actually the opposite is true. It takes more courage to be vulnerable than to hold back feelings. Vulnerability opens the heart, and to live life with an open heart is always the position of greatest strength.

32) Ride the waves

When we are in pain, it feels like forever. It's rarely forever. Pain comes and it goes. Sometimes it comes again. Then it goes again. Keep riding the waves as each one surfaces. This process takes time and courage, and is well worth the effort. Trust that there is a greater purpose at work here. Ultimately you will arrive at a new and better shore.

Smirking at the Green-Eyed Monster

It's Story Time...

"Randy, your words are like prescriptions and you choose them wisely."

What a nice compliment to hear from my friend, Carol. However, at the moment, I can't say I've always been so gracious.

After the amicable ending of one particular relationship, my thirty-six-year-old partner and I decided we still wanted to be friends. She then moved ten hours away and quickly found herself a new girlfriend...who just happened to be nineteen. They lived in a different state than I did, and I don't just mean geographically. The teenager was a serious writer of poetry who, despite her tender age, most definitely didn't approve of Eepster talk.

I felt a little bit weird about the fact that "they" were now a "them." It's not that I wanted to be in that relationship again. It's just that I got a slightly twinge-y feeling when my current ex talked about this new love. This new, almost-underage love. Does that make sense?

One time, she was trying to tell me something profound her new girlfriend had said. She was in the midst of saying to me, "I drove her to school and you know what she said?" and I blurted out, "Ice Cream Man! Ice Cream Man!"

It was such a mean thing to come out of my mouth; but I just couldn't help myself. Of course, I realize it's not nice to put other people down. I wouldn't have wanted someone to have made a joke about me at my expense. Perhaps if I'd felt more secure inside myself I wouldn't have made that horrible joke. I guess I just lost my grip. Perhaps I still need to develop some more maturity in this area.

"Sorry, new girlfriend. I didn't mean it." (Yes, I did). Oh well. Some of us have some more growing up to do; I won't name names.

Eventually the relationship between the two of them was youthanized. I can't honestly say I grieved about it. (Smirk.) Fortunately, my friendship with my ex stayed intact in spite of my ongoing stream of smart-ass remarks. And for that I am grateful.

Gratitude = A Great Attitude.

~~~ Steps to Happiness NOW! ~~~

33) Make an altar. Sacrifice your negativity

Taking your anger out on others—even if they "deserve it"—only breeds more of the same. The perfect thing to say when someone has taken their anger out on you is: "I hope you find much happiness in your life, because when people are happy, they treat others better." Think about living your life so that every one of your thoughts leads back to love.

34) Kiss your letters before you mail them—even the bills!

Every contact is an opportunity to put more love into the world. And each time you put love into the world, you'll feel better. Remember, the people who work for the phone or electric company are just like you and me. Draw a smiley face or write a kind word on the outside of the envelope just to brighten their mostly boring day. Even kiss your parking tickets!

35) Clean out the clutter in your mind

"Cleanliness is next to Godliness," and a squeaky clean mind is a good thing. Write down everything that is bothering you. This will help put your mind at rest and make things feel more manageable. Actually, according to Webster's, "cleanliness" is next to "cleanse" and "cleaner," not "godliness"; however, I'm sure you get the point.

36) File it under "healing"

Keep a file folder called, "Healing." If there's a situation that's upsetting you and cannot be resolved immediately, write it down and place it in your "Healing" file. This will free up your mind so you don't have to continually keep all the thoughts, facts, and figures circulating in your head.

Simultaneous Realities and the Importance of Hyphens

It's Story Time...

My friend Oshara and I devised a communication technique which works for two people who are living on the same planet and experiencing very different realities while trying to relate to each other.

We take the kitchen clock off the wall and put it between us. I say, "Go." She talks about whatever is on her mind for fifteen seconds while I monitor the time. At the end of fifteen seconds I say, "Stop." She stops even if in midsentence, and tells me to "Go."

Then I talk about whatever is on my mind, which may or may not have anything to do with what she's talking about, while she monitors my time for fifteen seconds. At the end of my fifteen seconds, she says, "Stop." I say, "Go," and then she picks up where she left off. We keep alternating like this, sometimes for hours.

EXAMPLE

Go. Randy: My friend Janice is really in a horrible divorce battle. Her husband is trying to steal the copyrights on her books and get full custody of their kid. She's freaking. I don't think I ever want to get married. *Stop*.

Go. Oshara: When people get divorced and have hyphenated names, if it was a really bad battle, all they might get in the settlement is the hyphen. You know, I really need to get my hair styled. I'd look so much better if . . . *Stop*.

Go. Randy: I don't know if I'll ever get over that last relationship I was in. I don't ever want to go through that level of pain aga . . . *Stop*.

Go. Oshara: How do I look? (Fluffs hair and looks in mirror.) Can you see how much better I'd look if my hair was poofier? *Stop*.

You see, it *is* possible for two people to maintain their separate crises and have a conversation at the same time.

Who says there's no such thing as a parallel universe?

~When Communication Heats Up~

Oshara and I weren't always this sophisticated in our ability to communicate. We were more like low-slinking reptiles when we were first in a relationship some years earlier. We had to work our way up the evolutionary scale to get to where we are now.

In the Amphibian Age we hissed at each other and made grimacing faces when we got angry.

As we evolved, we developed new tools. In the Stone Age, I threw things. If I didn't get my way, or if I felt hurt, I'd fly out of control. Actually I'd let other things fly out of control—like Chinese takeout or a glass jar of pennies flung at a door.

Sometimes I still revert to the Stone Age, but in a more conscious way. I like to throw eggs. I do it way out in nature, and they're not aimed at another person. I'll go buy twelve dozen eggs and let the checkout person at the grocery store think I'm making quiche. Then I go to my favorite egg-throwing rock and launch.

(Not too many people walk by the rock. Occasionally a hiker comes by. I've noticed that women think it's great and cheer me on with enthusiasm. Men go by quickly without commenting.)

Next, Oshara and I took a grand leap up the evolutionary scale. We learned language. Specifically, name-calling. In the middle of a fight, Oshara once screamed at me, "You're a manipulative jerk." And I screamed back at her, "I am not a jerk!"

We both stopped fighting and started laughing. I never denied being manipulative. I'm not manipulative. I just like to get my way. Because I'm right and I know what's best for everybody, all the time—just like you. (This was the Age of Reason.)

During the Age of Reason, we used humor to resolve our issues. One time we were in the car, and Oshara was at the wheel. We were headed down a busy city street when she had to slam on the brakes because the car in front of us had stopped and we were about to kiss its back end. She missed hitting the car by a sliver. This time I screamed at her, "Will you pay attention!" And she replied slowly and deliberately, "Randy, I've paid and paid. Don't I own it by now?" End of problem.

As we advanced into the Industrial Age, we discovered the telephone had more features than the phone company knew about. We assigned new designations for the keys on the number pad.

If Oshara said something that hurt my feelings, I'd say, "Press 3." Number 3 was the apology button. If I felt really hurt, she'd have to press it a whole bunch of times. Number 5 stood for "F*** You!" I don't remember the rest of the numbers. At the time I guess those were the important ones.

The Computer Age upped our evolutionary communication patterns even more. Once we went hi-tech, if she said something she wished she hadn't, she'd just hit the delete key on her forehead and delete it till it was all gone.

Now we're in the New Age. In the New Age, Oshara and I don't say anything bad about ourselves, each other, or anyone else. Here's what we do. If one of us slips and says a no-no about ourselves or the other, we give the other person a quarter. If we say something judgmental about anyone else, that goes for a dime.

The other agreement is we are not allowed to use the money we've collected to pay up. We have to use fresh money, so it's not the same dime and quarter passing between us.

Oshara stocks her winnings in front of a tiny laughing Buddha. I place mine in front of a picture of a poor supplicant, kneeling with outstretched arms at the feet of archangel Raphael.

I think Darwin would be proud. It only took Oshara and I four years to make such an evolutionary leap in our communication abilities. Perhaps letting go of judgments was the missing link we'd been searching for all along.

Your words are a powerful tool. Use them wisely for the biggest payoff.

~~~ Steps to Happiness NOW! ~~~

37) Zip your lip and bring your ear near

To be heard is one of the greatest gifts we can receive. To listen is one of the greatest gifts we can give. However, listening with full attention is currently on the Communication Skills' Endangered Species List. Listen more than talk and never interrupt unless your water breaks or someone is about to be bitten by a snake.

38) Whoa, slow down, Trigger

In conversation there is often a tendency to jump in as soon as the last words are leaving the other person's mouth. When one finishes sharing, sit in silence for just a second. Pausing honors the person who has spoken and allows her words to settle. You can still have your say and make all your important points, just give it a little space.

39) Put a cork in it

If one person is dominating a conversation, you might want to say, "I notice your mouth is running nonstop. Will you shut up already so I can speak?" Say it a lot nicer, though. Maybe something like, "I can see you're really on a roll, but I'm noticing I'm feeling a little left out. Could I have a turn too?"

40) Honor each other's needs

If some big storm cloud just blew your job or relationship away, you might need or want time focused solely on you. Ask the other person if he is available to hear what you're going through. This honors his needs as well as your own. It's good to check this out so the understanding is clear before you launch into your drama.

A Petty Confession, a Pop Quiz, and a Pack of Trident

It's Story Time...

I have a small confession to make—not the kind you hold in your guts thinking God will judge you for when you die. It's just a petty confession, probably assigned to some minor saint instead of an archangel.

Okay, here it is: I'm afraid of taking physical risks—I have trust issues. And besides, I might get a boo-boo. This probably relates back to the time I got dropped in a trust circle. Yes, it's true! I really did get dropped in a trust circle.

It was one of those weekend workshops—you know, the kind where you get empowered to be the master of your destiny, the queen or king of your universe and a victim no longer.

As I stood humbly in the middle of a circle, seven people lovingly looked into my eyes, each assuring me of their support with the words, "Randy, I am here for you."

I felt so safe, so supported. So I shut my eyes, and keeping my feet together on the floor, let myself fall like a tube of light into their waiting arms. Tenderly they passed me around the circle, loving hands supporting my weight. Gently they passed me to the right, to the left, to the right again, and then...Bam! No one was there and I hit the floor.

Moral: Just when it felt safe, the bottom fell out.

Although she was never dropped in a trust circle, my friend Debi has her own set of issues around trust. So she's devised a simple, brilliant test to determine trustworthiness in others. Debi asks herself the question, "Do their words match their actions, and do their actions match their words?" She listens to what a person says, then she watches to see how he follows through.

I've conducted the Debi test a billion—or at least seven—times in my interactions with people.

What about you? Could you pass the Debi test? Are you trustworthy? Do you honor your agreements? Do your words match your actions? Do your actions match your words?

POP QUIZ—THE DEBI TEST

Pick the answer you think best fits for each example:

1. Let's say you borrow $100 from a friend and you promise to pay her back by next Friday. Next Friday comes. Your friend calls and asks you where the money is. You say...

   A. Ha-ha, I changed my mind. Tough luck, sucker.
   B. OOPS, I forgot.
   C. I'm sorry, I'll have it for you next week. I promise.

   Or do you...

   D. Do what you promised and pay up when you said you would.

2. In the previous example, if you picked D, let's say now you've made plans to spend the following Tuesday with that same friend. If you chose some other letter, then make it a different friend, because that friend is probably no longer speaking to you. Anyway, now it's Tuesday and you've got menstrual cramps and diarrhea and you don't feel like going anywhere. Do you...

A. Ignore the phone when your friend calls and hope she goes away.
B. Rent videos.
C. Call your friend first and tell her you've got cramps and diarrhea and don't feel like going anywhere.
D. Take a couple of Midols, call your friend, and say you're on your way.

This is a trick question; be careful. I know you really want to rent videos, however that's not the best answer. However, it could be the next best answer after you do the first best answer. You might think the correct answer is again choice D. It isn't.

The best answer is C. The Truth of the Now outweighs the Commitment of the Then. This doesn't mean it's okay to flake out on your agreements. It just means it is important to always speak the truth as best you know it and to follow through as best you can.

Don't worry. Your friends will still like you, and they will respect you even more. They know they can count on you to always speak your truth. If they don't like you and don't respect you when you speak your truth, it's time to find some new friends.

So how did you do on the Pop Quiz? Did you get all the answers right? If you did, great! You can be proud of yourself. If you didn't, get out and meet some new people, because you're not going to have your old friends much longer.

If you passed the test, you may skip the following example and move to the next story. If you didn't pass the test, here's your chance to try again.

BONUS QUESTION

You're a new employee at a department store. Since all the department stores are being bought out or going under, you know you won't be there for long. Your boss sets you up by leaving a five-dollar bill at the cash register. You know you're being set up to see how you'll handle the situation.

Do you…

A. Tell your boss someone left a five-dollar bill on top of the cash register.
B. Slip the bill into your pocket along with some packs of Trident.
C. Slip the bill into your pocket without the packs of Trident.
D. Run outside and give it to the Salvation Army Santa if he promises to quit ringing the darn bell.

Think carefully before choosing your answer. Your integrity is at stake. Let's look at the consequences for each of the above actions. If you chose A, you are a moral person with high integrity. If you chose B, you are scum. If you chose C, you are scum without gum.

If you chose D, it could go either way. Either your boss sees you running out of the store and thinks you will never come back because you have struck it rich by finding that five-dollar bill, or in the best case scenario, your boss realizes you know how to think fast on your feet, so you receive a promotion because he hates the darn bell, too.

Of course, you only get to enjoy your promotion for two weeks until the store closes and you have to go off to find some multilevel marketing product to push on all your friends.

Tell the truth all the time—it's the best answer to any pop quiz Life throws you.

~~~ Steps to Happiness NOW! ~~~

41) Taking charge of your life does not mean you should run up another charge card

Taking charge of your life means you no longer blame others for your experience. It means you are willing to be honest with yourself and to express your truth in each moment. It means you know what your needs are and then express them while honoring and respecting other's needs as well. And it means you are also willing to take action.

42) Quit whining, it's not pretty

Catch your words as they fly out of your mouth. It's one thing to garner support under difficult circumstances, it's quite another to whine ad nauseam about your miserable life. At some point even your dog is going to put its paws over its ears and hide under the bed to escape your indefatigable complaining.

43) Focus on the positive

Remember the Universal Law of Attraction: Whatever you're thinking or feeling, you attract more of the same. Whine and you'll keep on drawing misery to yourself and wonder why. Feel hopeful and, unless your hopes are stomped into the ground, notice the increasing amount of good things coming your way.

44) Lies grow like flies

Never lie—not even little lies. And don't withhold information. If something needs to be said, say it. The more you express the Truth, the more your life will no longer be a lie. It takes vigilance to live a life of Truth. As you do it, it gets easier, and eventually it becomes fun, because the Truth always leads to a happier Now.

Poop Is a Very Proud Thing

It's Story Time...

Do you remember being potty-trained?

The other day, I was talking with a friend about our earliest childhood memories. Mine was lying down next to my very pregnant mother in my little twin bed. She asked me if I wanted to feel the baby kick. I said, "Yes," and she took my hand and placed it on her belly. I remember feeling my brother's little kicks as I rested my hand ever-so-gently on her belly so I wouldn't somehow accidentally "squish" the baby. I was around two and a half years old at the time.

My friend, a successful medical practitioner, told me about her earliest memory, which was taking her first poop in the toilet all by herself. She was so proud, she called her mother to come and see. Unfortunately, there was all this toilet paper in the way of a great view, so she fished out all the poops and lined them up on the edge of the sink.

Another friend said that once when she was four, she was very constipated. One day her mother was downstairs with a group of "society ladies" when the great moment of relief finally arrived. My friend came down the stairs and proudly displayed her wares with the comment, "Mommy, look, I made a whole dishful." What a proud moment. (She gets the credit for naming this piece.)

Let's face it, everyone poops. You and I poop. And poop smells. Of course, my poop doesn't smell as bad as your poop. It couldn't possibly. I'm too nice. Nice girls don't have smelly poop. If you're a nice girl, you don't have smelly poop either. All the boys have smelly poop. And some nice girls. Just not me. Sorry, that's the way it is.

Just in case you're one of the nice girls who has smelly poop or if you happen to be a boy, then you can learn a lot from Oshara.

Oshara and I used to work together. We ran a magazine. She started it. I finished it. No. It finished me. It finished her too. It was a magazine trying to help shift the consciousness on this planet. I'm writing about poop now. See where it got me?

Anyway, Oshara taught all new employees the rules for appropriate bathroom procedure. Picture this brand new, quivering-in-his-boots employee, intent on making a good first impression. And now picture Oshara holding a lighter and an incense stick, shouting from the bathroom doorway, "If you make a big stinky, use this."

To picture this correctly, let's use you as an example. You can be the brand-new, quivering-in-your-boots employee. You've quivered before. There you are, intent on being Mr. or Ms. Professional Magazine Person in your nice rayon suit you bought especially for your first day at work, and there's Oshara, publisher and owner in tie-dyes standing down the hall in the doorway of the bathroom, in front of three other employees at their desks, shouting to you about lighting big stinkies.

Since you don't know what Oshara looks like, it might be hard to picture this scenario correctly, so I'll give you more clues. Let's make the lighter a blue Bic. And the incense can be Nag Champa. If you don't know what Nag Champa smells like, then it can be strawberry. Just don't choose patchouli, because

I don't like patchouli. Now imagine Oshara is holding these things. The lighter would be in her right hand and the incense would be in her left hand because she's right-handed.

To get an idea of what Oshara looks like, picture someone who you think would say something like that. Oh, you need more clues? She's tall and thin like me. And she's extremely funny like me. She wears tie-dyes and I don't. That's the only difference. Now try to picture her. Great, that's more like it.

Stop quivering. You can take off your boots now. Someone else makes big stinkies. You don't. And even if you did make a big stinky in your life—either physically or metaphorically—so what? Can you accept yourself, big stinkies and all? Actually, your poop smells like roses so you don't have to worry. Mine does too. Isn't that better? Good. Now go pick some roses and give them to someone you love.

More Bodily Functions— ~~the Power of Positive Peeing~~

Poop may be a proud thing, but pee is a powerful thing.

I have a philodendron that I rescued from a job ten years ago. When I first inherited "Phil," he had two spindly little stalks and was about twenty inches tall. In ten years he reached the ceiling. Then something dreadful happened. One by one his leaves started turning yellow and falling off.

In spite of all my best intentions, over the years this phenomenon seemed to happen to a lot of my plants. For example, my outdoor porch was littered with the remains of dead spider plants, dead flower stalks, and weeds of every variety, which had overtaken any of the remaining healthy plants which had managed to survive thus far.

Oshara, who surrounds herself with a lush forest of greenery even in the tiniest of apartments, has often accused me of running a plant hospice where plants go to make their transition.

"But Oshara, I love this plant! What can I do to save him?"

"Let it die, Randy. It wants to move on to the light."

"Let him die? I can't let Phil die!" Phil had been transplanted into a much larger pot about a year ago. I didn't think he was over- or underwatered. The plant store had no advice. It was devastating to watch Phil wither away leaf by leaf. Then one of my friends suggested I pee in the plant.

At first this seemed really weird, but Phil was dying and nothing else was working. I found a wide-rimmed glass jar in the recycle pile and made it my official peeing jar. For eight months, that's all Phil drank. His leaves turned a rich, vibrant green. He was healthy and happy once again.

The only down side was that Phil lived in the corner next to my bed and sometimes my bedroom smelled like one of those city streets where someone regularly pees on the sidewalk. Outside of that, I was happy and so was Phil.

When Good Pee Goes Bad— ~~~the Power of Negative Peeing~~~

Dogs in Tiburon, California, have also demonstrated the power of peeing, but not with equally positive results. Recently that town installed an expensive, low-to-the-ground lighting system along the sidewalks in its trendy downtown area. Unfortunately, the low lights attracted every dog in the Western hemisphere, or at least every dog that made its way through Tiburon. Pretty soon every single light had been short-circuited by dogs peeing on the wires. Now the town is installing yet another expensive new system which is out of leg-lifting range.

Aim higher.

45) We are all the same underneath (although some of us have more body hair than others)

If you're constantly comparing yourself to others or are intimidated by them, remember, we all have the same bodily functions. Isn't that a charming thought?

46) There are no mistakes—only other opportunities to look foolish

You may not ever do or say things perfectly. That doesn't mean there's an out-of-order sign on your head. We try to be perfect, but we forget we are already perfectly ourselves. What else do we ever need to be anyway?

47) Let the corners of your lips turn into a smile

We need to laugh at our humanness more often. Lighten up. Practice smiling, then work up to laughing. It's good for your immune system and will keep away people who think you're weird.

48) Dare to be your most outrageous self

One person's proud moment can be an embarrassment for another. And so what? Put yourself out there. It's your life. Do it the way you want to. If you want to be outrageous, be outrageous. Each person responds to our actions in their own particular way. It is up to us to not be swayed by another's reactions in order to be true to ourselves.

If Men Are from Mars and Women Are from Venus, Where Does That Leave Me?

It's Story Time...

Don't be shocked.

I'm exploring the idea of eventually at some point in this decade being in a relationship with a man. Slowly and timidly, I am tiptoeing in that direction. I said tiptoeing—there are no other body parts involved. And currently, no men either.

This is a new, old thing for me. I was in love with a man once. I mentioned him right at the beginning of the book, remember? I was deeply in love. He asked me to marry him and we were going to ride off into the sunset together. He left at Thanksgiving. That was eleven years ago.

One day this past summer, as I opened the door to exit a restaurant, some guy walking by on the sidewalk looked over and said, "Hello, Randy." I looked at the man and didn't have a clue who it was. As I kept looking at him, I used my Rolodex brain to go through all the people it might be. Nothing was registering. Then, looking deeper into his eyes, all of a sudden it clicked.

Three thousand miles away, and eleven years later, my old boyfriend and I had just run into each other on a street in San Francisco. I was amazed, to say the least. This man I had loved and lived with, and had intensely grieved over for seven years, was standing in front of me, and I didn't recognize him. It was startling to come to the understanding that the man who I loved was twenty-nine years old, while this man standing in front of me was forty; he was a complete stranger.

He told me he'd ended our relationship because he was scared. We talked for about ten minutes and that was that. I gave him my business card thinking it would be nice to talk to him some more. He never called. And that's okay. A piece—no, let's make that a chunk—of my life came to completion in that moment. The pain from that ancient loss was now over. After eleven years I finally got the closure I needed to get on with my life.

So here I am, a free woman, free to explore my heart in relationship with men again. Free to begin again. Open to exploring new possibilities.

So what kind of person might I want to be with? Nowadays, people primarily rate each other by their looks. This doesn't seem right to me because: 1) beauty is subjective, and 2) it's a shallow and meaningless basis upon which to establish a relationship.

I think I can come up with a system for selection far superior to how people choose their partners today. My system will be fair because it will be objective. It will need to be totally measurable. I've got it! My system will be based on the ability to carry luggage.

Luggage is tangible. There can be no difference of opinion. You can look at the guy-person and see how much he can carry. You can even take a clipboard with you and make notes.

I'm an independent woman. I support myself, have a fax machine, and make my own lunches. There's very little I need from another human being. I just don't like to carry heavy things. And why should I when I can get some guy to do it?

My fantasy man will think nothing of lifting those five-gallon water bottles I can't budge. I'll look for a "six"—someone who can schlep six pieces of luggage simultaneously.

My ideal man probably has no neck or a very short, wide neck. (Statistics show that the shorter the neck, the more they can carry.) Then he can pick up two suitcases in each hand, have a pack on his back, and simultaneously balance some other package under his armpit.

That's my idea of a real man. Not only will he schlep all that stuff, he'll bring it up two flights of stairs. My place only has twelve steps up. However, I want to be prepared just in case I move.

My system will include bonus points, too. If the man initiates carrying something without being asked, he'll get double points, and if he's still carrying all that luggage after the first year of the relationship, he'll qualify for master points.

Actually I don't own six pieces of luggage. So let's make it grocery bags. Heavy grocery bags with lots of juice jars in them.

You can see how this is a fair system. It's a system everyone can agree on. "Yes, he's carrying six pieces of luggage (or grocery bags)," or "No, he's only carrying three pieces." Everyone can see.

I just shared my totally objective rating system with one of my male friends who immediately rated himself. He believed he was a "four." I didn't want to disappoint him, however, I'm sure he was just a "three." Poor guy.

If there's someone who's only a "two" or a "three," that's okay, because there's still another way he can score points. There'll be one more category: the ability to fix things. Faucet drips, hooking up the VCR, siphoning the waterbed, car anythings, or unclogging the pilot lights on the stove. Being able to fix stuff adds up to big, big points with me.

Triple points awarded if the person doesn't feel compelled to explain in great detail how he did it.

There. That's it. I think these are great ways to judge a likely candidate. Everything is fair and measurable.

Will the person stay? Will he work out his mother issues? Will he ever get off the couch? These issues can't be resolved at the beginning of a relationship. However, the ability to fix things and the willingness to carry luggage or grocery bags can be determined right from the start.

If the guy asks you what you're doing with a clipboard in your hand, just tell him you work for a survey company and you're asking all your neighbors about laundry detergent. No, I take it back. Don't lie. Never lie. Always tell the truth. Tell him you're researching a new possibility and leave it at that.

There are no guarantees, but there certainly are possibilities.

~~~ Steps to Happiness NOW! ~~~

49) Rejection is God's way of saying, "Don't settle for less"

If you've been rejected by someone in a love relationship, or rejected by anyone for whatever reason, know that there's nothing wrong with you. Understand that person is simply not the right person to bring you to your Highest Good.

50) Let go of the package that love must look like

These days, your knight in shining armor just might be wearing stainless steel. In a sermon at a New Age church some years ago, I remember the minister, Matt Garrigan, saying, "There are over five billion people on this planet, and you can't find someone to love you. Do you think you just might be a little too picky?" Let love in—especially when it comes in a form you might not have anticipated.

51) Search for the source

A friend asked, "When do the lessons get easier?" I replied, "When the heart knows its source." No other person is my source, therefore, even though I'm not in a relationship, I feel no lack of love. I've found the source of love inside myself, and my heart is full. I have plenty of love to give, so I'm giving it. This makes my Now much happier.

52) Collage your friends

If you want a partner with wonderful qualities, start by listing the best qualities of each of your friends. Then think of all the scumballs you have ever dated and list the opposite of their negative attributes. For example, rephrase, "I don't want to be with a man who doesn't hear a word I say," to read, "I want to be with a man who stops everything he's doing to listen to my every word—before he continues to load the washing machine."

Have You Seen My Job?

It's Story Time...

I've noticed I qualify for low-income phone services. I've noticed I'm afraid to spend five bucks on a burrito. I've noticed I don't like noticing what I'm currently noticing.

Realistically, what are my money-making options? Maybe the Fairy Job Mother will wave her magic wand and give me the job of my dreams, or worst-case scenario, I'll have to go find a job on my own. Oh lordy, lordy, this means I've got to go to work!

Now, we've already established that I am not a New Age Flake. It's not that I'm lazy either. I've put in more than my fair share of sixty-hour work weeks over the past ten years. Then why the bad attitude about finding a job? Think about your job. Then look in the mirror at the crow's feet which are forming around your eyes from all the times you've made gnarly faces at your boss behind his or her back. Or count how many bottles of Tums you go through in a week. Do I really need to explain it any further?

What might happen if we were to create a positive, life-affirming acronym for the word "job"? Maybe our attitudes about working might shift. Wait a minute. Who's "we"? I'm the one writing this. I'll have to create the acronym myself unless you get here in the next ten seconds. I'm counting. One-one thousand, two-one thousand, all the other one-thousands. Guess not. I waited. Okay, I'll do it myself.

J.O.B.—Joyful Overflowing a-Bundance. I like that. I want Joyful Overflowing a-Bundance. That's something I can get behind. Or in front of, or right in the middle of.

Jump in. You can have some too. We can all sit in a pile of a-Bundance. Doesn't that feel good?

What does your pile look like? Are you splashing around in a wagon full of money? Or maybe you're raking a big pile of leaves and all the leaves turn into ten-dollar bills. Then some neighbor kid starts playing in your pile, and you kick him out because you don't want to share. After all, it's your yard and all those leafy ten-dollar bills are yours.

Then you remember that with true a-Bundance there's enough for everyone. So you invite the neighbor kid back and say, "Here kid, take some of these, there's enough for everyone."

The kid says, "Golly gee, Mr. Galumpa, there's enough a-Bundance here for everyone." And he learns an important lesson.

And then the kid grows up and when he's out in his yard raking his leaves, he rakes them into the next yard to remind his neighbor that a-Bundance is to be shared.

Each of us has a different version of what true a-Bundance is. So, what does a-Bundance look like to me? Dessert. I mean, a dessert I can actually eat. This might not seem like a big thing to you. It is for me.

How would you feel if you were allergic to dairy, soy, wheat, mushrooms, yeast, vinegar, and any form of sugar? What if you were raised kosher-style and therefore couldn't eat piggily wiggilies or any type of shellfish? Think about a dish you like to make. Could you and I both eat it? Probably not.

For the first time in many, many years though, I am experiencing abundance in my food options in spite of all those things I can't have.

It's all because of Alan. Alan is a new friend. In addition to knowing all kinds of alternative health systems, he is also a cook. That's what he calls himself. I call him a vegetarian culinary specialist.

Even with my "Nope-Can't-Eat-That" checklist, Alan is able to give me millions of ideas of new things I can make. Now I'm cooking Thai dishes and Indian dishes and I just made a cornbread using his suggestions. Cornbread—that's my dessert. I am ecstatic about cornbread. To me, this is Joyful Overflowing a-Bundance.

In the past, I'd been told, "The only thing you can eat is dill and dirt." Now because of Alan, I can add rice milk or corn elbows or ginger to my dill and dirt. It's getting better all the time.

Aren't you happy for me? Now I can even come to dinner at your house. Let's pretend you want to invite me. Okay, go ahead. I'm so excited. I've heard you're a good cook. Start with dill and dirt. Now add something good to it. I can hardly wait. So what's for dinner?

Or maybe we could do a potluck. I'll bring the dill. You bring the dirt. If it comes out good, we could even market it. "Dill and Dirt, the tasty treat that's crunchy to eat." It has a certain flair, a je ne sais quoi, don't you think?

I want to nurture this newfound a-Bundance. I want to take it for walks. Play with it in the park. Invite you over to share it with me.

Let's face it, though, right now I really need to put my attention on finding a J.O.B. to support myself. So let's see what's in the paper.

Here's one. "Regional Coordinator—Find volunteer musicians to play for hospitalized children, homeless people, and other groups all over the Bay Area." I have the skills they're looking for and this sounds like fun.

My friend Debi comes over. She's job-hunting too. Although we have different work backgrounds, she's equally qualified, and I think she'd also be excellent for the position, so I encourage her to apply for it too.

She's hesitant. She says she doesn't want to jeopardize my chance of getting it. As Oshara taught me years ago, there is absolutely no competition. Competition is just another way of saying you believe in lack. In actuality, there's a perfect place for her and there's a perfect place for me. We all have our perfect place in this universe. This place may be my perfect place, or it may be hers. If it's not perfect for me, then something better is meant to be. And the same goes for her.

I guess something better was meant for both of us, because neither of us got it.

My friend Talia is encouraging me to create my own job. With what? She says, "Talk to God. Be receptive to what you hear."

So God and I are talking. God thinks I should send out more resumes. I'm negotiating for a little more time to finish writing the book. God thinks I'll have more material once I start working again. So we're going round and round with this. I think God will see it my way. I'll tell you how it goes.

Spirit's opened up a bank account in your name—draw on it.

~~~ Steps to Happiness NOW! ~~~

53) If you've got money fears, spend a day at the beach

Let's pretend every grain of sand at the beach is a dollar. Go gather up a pile of sand and make it really big. Do you have enough? Make it even bigger. Make a giant mountain out of sand. Now do you have enough? Do you need to guard your sand mountain or is your supply unlimited? Is there enough for everybody to make a giant sand pile or just you?

54) Life's much more sweet when you don't compete

The quality of our Now is determined by who we are and how we live our lives in this moment. People who compete only live their lives in fast-forward. Go faster. Go faster. More RAM for the computer. Make it go faster so we can go faster. Guess what? We are not machines. We're not innately programmed to live in fast-forward.

55) Surround yourself with the ocean of abundance

When I started getting freaked about money, I wanted to change those fear thoughts fast. So first, I painted a personal prosperity angel on silk. Then I went to the ocean to surround myself with "the ocean of abundance." And lastly, instead of saying, "I'm almost broke," I'm proudly stating, "I'm in the phase before I make my first million." There, that feels much better. You can do this, too.

56) Being poor is a state of mind, so move to a different state

One of my friends recently sent me a check for a hundred dollars with the message, "I don't want to see you starve on my shift." She gave freely from her heart as if she was rich, even though she currently lives in a house without heat. (She's also in the phase right before she makes her first million.) No matter what her financial status, my friend will never be poor. How about you?

I Just Made a Happy Meal Out of My Finger

It's Story Time...

One evening, I wanted to make stew for dinner. I was in the kitchen slicing onions with a large butcher knife when, all of a sudden, the knife took off my skin instead. Darn. Don't you just hate when that happens?

I hightailed it over to an emergency room, my thumb carefully wrapped in a kitchen towel and elevated over my head as I drove. When I walked into the urgent care facility, I was helped by the kindest, sweetest people I've ever met in the medical profession. They smeared some tire patch on my booboo thumb—they insisted upon calling it a laceration—then wrapped it in wads of gauze until it looked like a giant banana.

I was touched by the obvious feeling of warmth among those people. Not only did they seem to genuinely like each other, they also worked well together, and most of all, appeared to sincerely care about their patient—me!

This doesn't seem to be the norm in most work environments. You know what I mean. As my friend Debi says, "Most businesses fall into the category of 'dysfunction stew'."

Recipe: DYSFUNCTION STEW

Sauté three employees with seniority who don't do diddly squat.

Stir in one employee who really knows how to make things work but doesn't have the power within the organization to do so.

Gradually fold in two workers who possess the communication skills of slugs unless it comes to reporting someone.

Add a heaping tablespoon of complaining customer.
Bring to boil.

Marinate with an ounce of know-it-all boss who never shows appreciation for anything.

Sprinkle with a dash of gossip. Simmer.

For stronger flavor, let sit overnight and stew.

Supervisors love to dole out heaping portions of dysfunction stew. In fact, they often create the recipe from scratch. And even if they didn't create it, most of them still love to give that pot a good stir.

~~~A Heapin' Helpin' Just for Me~~~

In the early Eighties I worked at a pit of an institution. It's now defunct; back then it was just dysfunct. About once a week, my supervisor made sure to whip up a special dysfunction stew just for me. What a gal. Stir that stew pot! Stir that stew pot!

One time, two coworkers and I were pushing three people in wheelchairs through a field of snow-covered weeds so they could go horseback riding. Once we were finally inside the riding rink, we had to drag the wheelchairs a long way through soft dirt to reach the special ramps so they could mount the horses.

I don't know if you've ever pushed a wheelchair through snow, weeds, or soft dirt. If you have, then multiply that by three. Just in case this is something you've never done, this was the kind of assignment for which people deserve medals or at the very least, a truss. This was heavy-duty dedication.

Later that day, we returned to the institution, tired, sore, and happy, because it had been a good experience for our people. The very next morning, however, the supervisor confronted me.

"I had a complaint there was hay on the van when you returned from the riding rink."

"What, no medal?" I thought. As trivial as it might seem, for someone to register a complaint like this at this institution was very serious, as the consequences meant having this complaint filed in one's permanent record. Now it was certainly possible that a few strands of hay from the rink could have twisted themselves into the spokes of the wheels on the wheelchairs. But it couldn't have been more then a few strands, otherwise we would have noticed it.

This was her thousandth bogus confrontation with me and I simply decided, no more stew. I'd had enough. I looked at Madam Lovely very seriously, then confessed.

"Hmmm. Hay on the van. Yes. I was playing Baby Jesus in the Manger."

Then I turned around and went about my business.

I don't know where that came from. I had never talked to anyone like that before. It felt great. She walked away with a puzzled expression on her face, not knowing quite how to respond. I was sure I was going to get fired. She didn't fire me.

About a month later, I quit. After all, there's always more stew to sample in the world.

~~~~~ Forgiving the Cook ~~~~~

About three years later, I had another boss who made that supervisor seem like a mere prep cook. This guy swore and threw recipes in people's faces. He intimidated, lied to, and insulted the staff. This guy was not my choice for "Employer of the Year."

Almost every day, I'd leave my desk and go outside to cry after he'd delivered one of his tirades. Even though he was pretty obnoxious, I didn't quit. I loved the work and I needed the big seven bucks an hour I was making. I also hung in there for another reason. This man was ill and I thought if I could just hang on, I might be able to outlast him. I was right. Somehow I endured, and he died about a year and a half later.

Over time, I've done many forgiveness exercises to release him. I could feel forgiveness happening, however, like an onion, there were always more layers to unpeel. Until recently.

I saw this man in a dream, standing in a classroom in front of a blackboard. I remarked to myself, "He's teaching me something." Just as I said that, I received a tremendous transmission of love from him. My heart filled with the most beautiful feeling. It was an experience I cannot easily put into words.

I know from that experience that whatever he needed to heal in himself, he has. And he has made his amends with me as well. Everything has been transformed back to Love in its purest essence. Now there is nothing left to forgive. The stewpot is buried once and for all. And I learned that at the heart of all beings, there is love.

Bury the stewpot.

57) Sometimes when you think you've failed, you've actually graduated

If you've given it all you've got and things don't work out your way, you have not failed. There were reasons for the experience regardless of the end result. Perhaps you learned the lessons you were supposed to learn, and this is the Universe's way of telling you, "Now it's time to move on; you've got a brand-new degree to earn somewhere else."

58) Be an angel in your past

Sometimes when I recall painful memories from the past, I imagine myself as an angel. I embrace that former Self which experienced so much pain and I comfort her. With full knowing, I tell her that in time things will work out and I hold her to my heart as she weeps. Be very gentle with your sweet Self, in the past, present, and future. Loving yourself is essential to your healing.

59) Forgive the past; it can't hurt you anymore

When we hold someone in a place of anger or hatred, we put her in a prison in our minds where she can no longer hurt us. The truth is, the one who is imprisoned is oneself, forever chained to the other in a bond of victimization or anger, until we can resolve it within ourselves or with her.

60) Life always moves us toward a greater good

Pretend it's five years ago and a psychic is telling you what you will be doing five years in the future (Now).

Imagining yourself then, could you believe your current reality would be what it is now? I couldn't have foreseen I would grow into the place where I am now. However, life moved me forward just the same.

Living Uncensored

It's Story Time...

Let's pretend all of life is a true-or-false test and you are the one about to take the test. Get out your number two pencil and no looking at anyone else's answer. Ready? Okay. Here's your first question:

Are you being true to yourself?

Guess what? That's the only question on the test and you are the only one who can ever answer it. In fact, you have your whole life to answer it. You don't even need a number two pencil, just a willingness to look inside.

To look inside requires getting quiet and listening to your own inner voice. Years ago a seven-year-old girl once said to me, "I have a voice inside me that no one can hear, only me." Leave it to a seven-year-old to deliver one of life's greatest truths!

It took me years to hear my own voice. I thought I was hearing it once, then I found out I was actually hearing my mother's voice. Don't get me wrong, my mother's voice is a very nice voice. I love my mother's voice. It's just that my mother's voice is my mother's voice, not mine.

In order to hear my own voice, I discovered I had to tell the truth to myself and to others, and to start living my truth in every moment.

This was not something that happened easily or spontaneously. I didn't wake up one glorious morning, rub the sleep out of my eyes, then see the big bright sun shining through my window and state to the world, "I must tell my truth. Listen everybody, I must live my truth." It is a way of being which has evolved slowly over time.

If I felt hurt by either the words or actions of another, I used to melt into a little teeny-weenie puddle of low self-esteem and withhold telling him how his words or actions affected me. Then I'd notice that by not telling him how I really felt, a little part of my heart would close down; and with each little hurt, more and more distance would grow between us.

I made an agreement with myself. I decided as soon as I became aware of when I was consciously withholding speaking my truth to anyone, I would express it and let the other person know.

This seemed like a very risky thing to do, because telling the truth feels scary. Who knows what the consequences might be? I decided to do it anyway.

What happened, in fact, was instead of having the word "REJECTED!" stamped in big, bold, red letters across my forehead, an even deeper bond would typically form between myself and the other person.

Here's a magic technique for speaking the truth: Simply, "notice and report." For example, when someone has said something to me that has caused me to bristle, I notice what happens in my body as he says it. Then I report what I feel. That's all I do. I might respond with, "I could feel my stomach tighten when you said that. I'm feeling very shaky and unsure right now."

Giving feedback in this way has never put anyone on the defensive, because this kind of feedback doesn't make another person bad or wrong. You are simply reporting your own feelings and he gets to hear how his words or actions have affected you. He is free to respond in any way.

The bottom line is that I want to stay in my heart, or to come back to that place if I'm temporarily away from it. So how I report my feelings or which feelings I choose to report is crucial, if this is the result I am striving toward.

If I feel hurt by someone's actions, I don't jump on the phone and scream at her or cry so she'll know how much her actions have hurt me. The old Randy would have done that. Now I don't need for her to hear how much pain she has caused me.

Instead I sit back, feel the feelings as they arise, and calmly go inward and decide what action I want to take. What do I want? When I know the answer, I take the appropriate action. If I don't hear a clear answer, I do nothing. When an answer does not come, I've learned, more time, information, or life experiences are necessary before the answer appears.

For example, I received a letter from an advice-wielding, Bible-verse-spouting woman who was determined to tell me what I was doing "wrong" in my life. The letter was full of personal criticisms. As I read her letter my adrenal glands went into action. First I felt angry, then self-righteous. So I jumped on my computer and typed a two-page response, determined to let this woman know just how angry she'd made me.

Although it felt important to acknowledge my spit-and-venom feelings and express them, by the time I completed the letter, I was not feeling any greater degree of love for her. After all, self-righteousness and love cannot occupy the same space. Sending my "How dare you?" letter was not what would connect me back to love. And that was my goal.

So instead, I wrote her a handwritten note: "This doesn't feel very loving, except for the part at the end which says you love me. Please try again."

This note had no stingers in it. Happily, I mailed the note off and was able to let go of the incident immediately. How the woman responded was entirely up to her. The important thing was I had expressed my truth in a gentle way and was back in my heart. Two days later I received an "OOPS, I'm sorry" letter in the mail. End of incident.

Speaking the truth is a great way to let go of the victim stance. It's not that situations beyond my control won't ever happen; it's just that I keep learning new ways of handling things so I don't feel like a perpetual victim. I can notice how I feel, then choose how I want to respond.

This is a big step for someone who has always had a flair for the highly explosive and melodramatic. For years I would have been a perfect guest for Sally Jesse or Geraldo, but no more. Now I have a choice. So what do I choose? I choose to keep my heart open as much as possible. I choose to love people instead of hate them.

There are no perfect people, just perfect opportunities.

~~~ Steps to Happiness NOW! ~~~

61) It takes tremendous courage to live in truth

If I know a choice is not for my Highest Good and I make that choice anyway, nothing will go right in my life because I'm not in alignment with the flow of the Universe. For example, if a relationship consistently makes me unhappy no matter what I do, I know I'm not on the right track. Although jumping off might feel like hell, it's better than the consequences of staying in something I know is not best for me.

62) Face the scariest word on the planet

Why do we compromise ourselves? Because it feels safer than confronting that part of ourselves which knows the truth. Once the truth is spoken, change invariably follows. And "change" is one of the scariest words on the planet.

63) Learn the art of "non-compromise" in relationship

We often compromise ourselves in the guise of not wanting to hurt someone else's feelings. The truth is, when we compromise ourselves, nobody wins. I don't mean be selfish and never compromise. I'm talking about being true to your core.

64) Truth is the pathway to peace

When you speak your truth you are saying, "This is who I am." It's not about making someone wrong. It's simply about saying what is true for you and for you alone. Although speaking the truth may lead to a giant freefall, it always leads to inner peace as well.

Déjà Car Vu

It's Story Time...

My Honda Prelude has reached its fourteenth birthday. That's really old in dog years. This past season, Old Trusty has been in and out of the car hospital for numerous operations, as one by one the parts have been coughing up their last breaths. Dr. Kevorkian, please help!

No. No. I need my car. I can't afford another one right now. Please, start the IV in the gas tank right away. More meds! Give it more meds.

This past month, on the way into San Francisco, my car had a massive coronary. It was a serious attack and almost cost it its life. I had just started to cross the Golden Gate Bridge when, all of a sudden, I saw fumes pouring out the front end. Next I heard a tick-tick sound. Oh my God, its ticker was going.

I continued to drive across the bridge, listening to the steady ticking and watching the fumes head toward the ozone layer. The nearest gas station was a few miles away, so I decided to push the Fates and kept driving.

As I drove from block to block, each light turned red just as I reached it. And every time I had to stop at one of those darned lights, the car died. It would start up again only after much prayer work. Finally Old Trusty said, "Enough already," and pooped out at a really busy intersection.

I could see a gas station in the distance up the road. Prayer was not helping. The car would not start. Since its body had more potholes than a New York City street, I considered pushing my feet through the bottom of the frame and walking the car up the block to the station, like Fred and Barney might have. Then lo and behold—yes, lo and behold—it started up one last time. Somehow I made it into the jam-packed, tiny lot at the gas station, then Old Trusty immediately went into full cardiac arrest. That was that.

Rather abruptly, a mechanic asked me to move my car.

"It's dead, Jim. It's not going anywhere."

Looking annoyed, he sighed in aggravation and walked away. Next, the owner, a big burly guy covered with grease, came over. I described Old Trusty's symptoms to him.

"So, what do you want us to check?"

"Uh-oh," I thought to myself. "I don't know what tests to tell Doc Burly to order. Isn't he supposed to know? Isn't this why he went through years of training? I don't like icky car things."

Suddenly, I felt like my car was in the hands of Gomer Pyle's buddy, Goober. What could I do? It wasn't going anywhere. So I checked it into the hospital and ordered it vegetarian meals just in case that would help. Then I caught buses back to my home, a good hour's distance away, where I nervously awaited the results of the MRI.

Finally, the phone rang. "I've got bad news," the doc said. "You blew the head gasket. Your car needs to have a pacemaker installed if you want it revived. Seven hundred dollars and your old rust bucket will live to see another day."

Yikes. Seven hundred dollars! I had no income, and I was draining all my savings. Well, at least I had a credit card. I needed the car.

"Yes, hook up the lifeline."

The doc said the procedure would take seven to ten days. After a week went by, I called to see when I might be able to bring Old Trusty home. I couldn't. Some guy at the machine shop was on vacation that week and the pacemaker wasn't ready.

No one had called to tell me the operation had been postponed. I felt more anxiety. My car did not appear to be in the best of hands. What could I do?

I could look for another car doctor. One place, which was even further away, said they would do the job for $450. That was a big difference. I checked into ambulance fees. Towing Old Trusty to this hospital would be expensive. This other station had come highly recommended by a friend, so even if it was expensive, Old Trusty would be getting the quality care he deserved.

By now it was a Friday. I had borrowed a friend's car and was headed back home via the road where Old Trusty lay. I wanted to confront the station owner, arrange for the tow, and get my car out of there. The closer I got to the station, the more fear I felt. My car had been there for two weeks now. The doc would be upset to lose such an expensive repair job. Would he charge me a storage fee or tack on other expenses? Would he get angry and give me a hard time?

I felt highly intimidated. Here I was, a woman entering a greasy world where men with big power tools rule. I didn't know anything about cars and I was sure Doc Burly was a slick operator who was going to take advantage of my ignorance, as well as the fact that I am female.

"I know what I need," I said to myself, "I need testosterone. I need someone who can match that kind of energy. I need an alpha male!" I decided if I was going to confront the doc, I was not going to do it alone. I would ask one of my male friends to come with me. Breathing a sigh of relief, I drove on past the station.

"Now which male friend of mine has the kind of testosterone that can stand up to someone like Doc Burly?" I pictured all of my male friends. No name stood out among them. I have male friends who are sweet and kind and in touch with their feelings. None of them knows how to grunt.

The only one with the kind of testosterone this situation called for was my brother. He might not know much about mechanical doohickeys, but at least he has a deep, booming male voice and he isn't afraid to use it. I knew he would help me in a second, however, he lived clear across the country.

Then I thought of a friend who liked to imitate Howard Stern. I figured anyone who imitated Howard Stern had to have testosterone. "Howard" said he'd be happy to help me. Since it was Friday evening, we made plans to go to the station early Monday morning. Sunday night, the phone rang. It was "Howard." He had hurt his back. There was no way he could accompany me the following day.

Darn, where's the testosterone when I need it? I'm not in menopause yet, so I don't even have any chin whiskers to count on. What can I do?

Earlier that morning, a psychic had given me a message. I hadn't told her a thing about me. She had said there was a very large Native American guide who would protect me in a situation in which I felt insecure and afraid. Oh. So even though "Howard" couldn't help me, could I now relax knowing I had testosterone in spirit form?

Monday morning, I summoned all of my inner strength, as well as my alpha male spirit guide, and called the car hospital.

Doc Burly answered in a friendly voice, talking to me as though we were old friends.

"Hey, glad you called. We've got the part and we've been working on it. It'll be ready for you by Wednesday afternoon."

Well, so much for the confrontation. Since it was already being worked on, I decided to let them finish the job. Any other option seemed too complicated. All of that worry and concern about some future moment led nowhere. Old Trusty would be wheeled out of the hospital in just two more days.

On checkout day, the phone rang. "I've got bad news," said the doc. "The radiator's totally rusted through and water is seeping out the bottom. It's going to cost you another $320 to replace it."

I checked my back. There was no sign on it that said, "Kick me." I hung up the phone to think about my options. For the next hour, I burned up the phone wires and eventually found a discount radiator shop where I could get a rebuilt radiator for one hundred dollars less then what the Doc had quoted. I even found a repair person much closer to where I lived who would install it for eighty dollars less than the doc would. Then I called around to figure out a towing option. Unfortunately, I couldn't quite get that part to come together.

Earlier that morning I had been having such a wonderful time, writing. Now here I was enmeshed in all the phone calls and complications surrounding my car. Where did all of my joy and creativity go? I made a decision—enough hospital calls for one day. I would spend the rest of the day enjoying the process of writing. Tomorrow I would deal with the car.

So I let go of all the ditsy details and concerns about the car, went back to totally being consumed by the present moment, and worked on my story until it thrilled me.

The next morning I drove a friend's car to one end of San Francisco and bought the used radiator. Then I drove toward the other end of San Francisco where my car was convalescing.

I was a little scared of Doc Burly, so I prayed. I decided it wouldn't hurt me to call on my testosterone spirit guide to help, too. I wanted to ask the doc if he would come down in his estimate for the labor.

I also thought about a phrase I'd coined off the slogan, "Practice Random Acts of Kindness." I had recently started saying my own version, "Practice *Intentional* Acts of Kindness." I imagined the doc cared about me and was willing to help. I thought about him wanting to be kind to me.

Nervously, I pulled into the station. The doc was very friendly and actually seemed happy to see me. (Guess he must have been excited thinking about the big payment I was just about to make.) I showed him the radiator I'd found and told him about the mechanic who had offered to install it at the lower rate. I told him how I would not have fixed the car if I had known the radiator was shot in addition to the head gasket, because I could not afford to spend that amount of money.

As I spoke to Mr. Burly, I imagined he wanted to be kind. Then taking a breath, I took the risk and asked him if he would be willing to come down in price.

Amidst the noise of the busy station, he paused, put his hands to his lips and thought about it. Then he offered to do the job for just a wee bit more than what I had asked for, way below his original price. I was thrilled. Instead of seeing this horrible monster goober guy as I had originally projected, I saw someone who was kind standing next to me.

I was just about to say to him and to the woman behind the cash register, "There really are angels in the world"—meaning them—when I jumped, startled, and said, "Oh, my God."

He and the woman looked at me, wondering what had just happened. I told them I was just about to thank them for being angels to me when that very second, out of the corner of my eye, I saw a real live, giant angel statue sitting right there on their counter staring back at me with a big smile on its face.

So it was a powerful lesson for me in many ways. When I had first seen these people as bad guys, what came back to me was "bad guy" energy. Later, when I thought of them as angels, I received kindness, friendliness, caring, a drop in price, and even a big smiling angel looking at me. Also because I'd spoken up and done some research, I'd saved a total of $120 from the original quote.

I took care of myself, spoke up for myself, and allowed other people to be angels as well. Old Trusty came home and passed his monthly treadmill tests with flying colors.

Almost a year to the day after Old Trusty had first blown that head gasket, I was driving across the Golden Gate Bridge when white smoke started sputtering out of the back end. Sure enough, for the second year in a row, in the month of March, on the Golden Gate Bridge, Old Trusty had once again blown a head gasket. What were the odds?

This time Old Trusty couldn't even limp off the bridge. Of course this had to happen during the early morning commute as thousands of cars were heading into San Francisco only to fight for parking spaces once they got to the other side.

Since there was no curb, I shifted Old Trusty into neutral and managed to roll all the way down the bridge, thanks to the gentle arc of the span. Old Trusty came to a dead halt in front of the tollbooth station.

A booming voice over a microphone bellowed from inside. "Don't move!" (Like I really had a choice).

In a few minutes, a giant tow truck was behind me pushing Old Trusty off the exit ramp.

"Bye, Old Rusty Trusty. Off you go to that Great Superhighway in the Sky!"

The next day, I rented a mold-infested junker and went off in search of new wheels. Over the next month, I shook hands with every sleazy car dealer within a two-hour radius. And guess what? I found a really great car, a little sporty number with only 24,500 miles on it. It was even made in the same decade as the decade we were in! What a concept! There was one little problem. It was way out of my price range.

Weeks later I finally found a car with low mileage in my price range. Although it was not my "dream car," I was willing to settle for it. I was tired of looking.

A salesman gave me a quote and I told him I wanted to think about it over night. The next day I went back to get it. The salesman, who was salivating over his forthcoming commission, went off to file the necessary paperwork. After waiting for what seemed to be too long a time, he reappeared and told me he couldn't give me the car at the price he had quoted me. Today it was selling for $500 more. A different manager was on duty that day and he wouldn't let the car go for the amount the manager from the previous day had approved.

As I did a tailspin and headed for the door the manager came flying out of his office telling me what a great deal the car was even at the higher price.

"Bye-bye." I drove off.

Needless to say, I was bummed. The next day, I wound up back in the first lot where that spiffy white car was. Just for kicks, I test drove it again.

In the end, my parents decided to up their ante and help me get it. So even though I was willing to settle for the car I wasn't excited about at first, the Universe wouldn't give it to me. I wound up getting what I had really wanted all along.

It is now March of another year. My new car has been running great. However, every time I cross the Golden Gate Bridge, I still ask my car angels to watch over me, just in case.

Never settle. Go for what you really want.

~~~ Steps to Happiness NOW! ~~~

65) You may not have a choice over the hand you're dealt; however, you do have control over how you play it

If you're afraid to risk, you'll never know what the possibilities are. If you've expressed yourself without holding anything back and you've done everything you could possibly do to make something happen, you'll know you gave it your all. After that you can let it go. The outcome will be what the outcome will be. You will feel better, regardless.

66) If you don't know, find out

If you're feeling afraid or intimidated, get more information. This will help ease your fears. The more knowledge you have, the more empowered you'll feel. You don't have to be a know-it-all. You just have to know enough. If you don't know enough, find someone who does.

67) You don't have to go it alone even if it's one of those lessons where you have to do it all by yourself

Asking for support doesn't mean you're a wimp. Get all the support you need. Make a list of people you can call for such occasions. That way if you're needing to reach out, you don't have to spend hours thinking about who you could possibly dial. Also ask for heavenly assistance. Someone up there may be eagerly waiting to hear from you.

68) Choose your thoughts like your friends

We choose our friends because, hopefully, they are the kind of people we feel wonderful around and who bring out our best. Instead of seeing people as bad guys, start sincerely thinking of them as people who also have a best side. Either you'll be dreadfully wrong and regret ever having tried it, or they'll actually start treating you differently and you'll be amazed.

Did Beaver Cleaver Steal My Art?

IT'S STORY TIME...

F!%*ing, irresponsible hippies.

Ten years' worth of my artwork, my sacred mandalas, had vanished. The mandalas, each one having been painstakingly woven by hand, had been on display in a home as part of an art show.

One of the housemates had invited me to leave them up in the house after the show ended. It had seemed like an okay thing at the time. After all, it was a large household and many people visited; the perfect opportunity for more sales.

Six months later, I learned there had been a fire at that house. Not only that, prior to the fire, no one remembered having seen my artwork in the past four months.

What? No one had seen my artwork? There had been a fire? No one had called me?

First Response: Panic. Waves of adrenaline coursed through my veins. "Where's my artwork? My artwork's gone! What happened to it?"

Second response: Act. I started making phone calls to see if I could track down my work. Results: Two of the housemates were out of the country, one was somewhere in Southern California, and countless other people had moved in and out and through. Some phone numbers were already disconnected. Would I ever see my artwork alive again? More panic.

Third response: See if I can find my artwork myself. The house was open. The only one home was a young hippie woman who had named herself after an herb. She was staying there for the weekend. She gave me permission to go rummaging through the place.

I ran around like a madwoman on a mission to save her babies. I checked out every nook and cranny, running from room to room, opening closets, slamming doors, racing in every direction to rescue my precious artwork. I couldn't find my pieces anywhere.

Fourth response: Imagine the worst. My artwork had vanished. It was gone. I was sure I'd never see it again.

Fifth response: Cry. I didn't foresee this. This was totally beyond my control. I was a victim of this situation.

Sixth response (a three-parter): 1) Call friends—"Something terrible just happened!" 2) Get support and sympathy—"Randy, we're so sorry. Is there anything we can do?" 3) Cry some more—"I can't believe it!"

Seventh response: Clench teeth, get ripping angry, and feel justified about it. These people had removed ten years' worth of my identity as an artist. I had put over a thousand hours of work into those mandalas. No one had even bothered to call me. Imagine a cartoon character with steam coming out of its ears. That's me.

Eighth response: Name-call. "F!%*ing, irresponsible hippies. F!%*ing, totally irresponsible hippies." I said it over and over. It quickly became my new mantra.

Ninth response: Call a psychic friend. "Your artwork is safe. It's just going to take some time before you get it back." A ray of hope emerged.

Finally, the tenth response: Calm down. I realized I would (hopefully) get my mandalas back.

Although I would have preferred to solve this problem as quickly as possible, I could see this one would have to play itself out with its own sense of timing. Glumly, I went back to my daily routine.

Within a few weeks, the housemates began to resurface and I started making more calls to track down my art. The results:

1) Beaver thought Wally took my stuff down and put it somewhere.

2) Wally thought Eddy did it.

3) Eddy thought Mrs. Cleaver did it.

4) Mrs. Cleaver blamed it on Ward.

In other words, none of them knew where my artwork was, and furthermore, none of them had anything to do with it. Still, all of their fingers seemed to be pointing in the general direction of the basement.

I had briefly looked in the basement the day of my madwoman search. The basement was a pitch-black space with a dirt-based floor. One of the walls was partly exposed to the outdoors. The basement served as the storage space for all of the housemates and God knows who else. It would have been easier to go searching for my artwork at the town dump.

Another panicky thought entered my mind. If my mandalas were indeed down there, had they survived the storms these past months, or were they sitting somewhere in a soggy box, soaked and covered with mildew? Back to the mantra:

"F!%*ing, irresponsible hippies. F!%*ing, totally irresponsible hippies."

What could I do with this rage? I was so angry at the Cleavers. None of them seemed to care whether I found my art or not. I wanted them to know how upset I was at them.

I plotted a revengeful fantasy. An eye for an eye. I'd take Wally's gray parrot and Beaver's conga drums. I'd take Eddy's van and June's beaded earrings. I'd go through their rooms and just help myself. Then they'd know what it felt like to suddenly lose something of deep personal value. I'd keep their precious, meaningful possessions as collateral until I got my own precious and meaningful artwork back.

It was a great fantasy. I squinted my eyes and hunched my shoulders with vengeful pleasure as I thought about it. Of course, I had no intention of carrying it out. My conscience wouldn't allow me to act that way. Damn. Morals. Besides, that wasn't what I really wanted.

All I wanted was to have my mandalas back. Suddenly, it occurred to me that I didn't have to teach anyone a lesson. Nor did I need to impress upon them how upsetting their lack of response to me felt. I just wanted my art back. One more time, I called the house.

"Hello, Wally. This is Randy."

"Hey, girl, how ya doing?"

(Girl? I feel my teeth clenching.) "Wally, did you ever get my phone call about a month ago?"

"Oh, yeah. I was out of the country. I was gonna call you."

(Right, yeah, uh-huh.) "Do you have any idea what happened to my artwork?"

"I heard it's in the basement. You know, we're having a party this weekend, it's gonna be great, you should come."

(I am going to kill. I'm talking about my precious artwork, and he's talking about a party.) "Well, I'm not feeling in a party mood right now. I just really want to get my artwork back."

"Hey, I'll help you look for it. I'm sure it's here somewhere. When do you want to come over?"

(My ears perk up like a dog about to be thrown a biscuit. He's really offering to help? Does he mean it?) "How about tomorrow around 2:00?"

"Great. Just call me first."

(Not trusting he'll follow through) "I'll call around 1:00 tomorrow."

We said our good-byes and hung up. Would he really be there? My guess was he wouldn't. So many people in that house had already let me down, I didn't expect him to keep his word. But he did. By the time I drove up their driveway, I was beginning to feel hopeful.

However, they'd just blown a fuse in the house, and now there was no source of light in the basement.

What? Yet another obstacle? Instead of blowing an internal fuse myself, I decided to remain hopeful and positive and went to get a flashlight out of my car. I also told Wally how thankful I was that he was willing to help me.

In an instant, I traded in the seething, self-righteous anger I'd felt toward all of them for a genuine feeling of gratitude and appreciation. When I did this, I no longer saw a "f!%*ing, irresponsible hippie" standing in front of me. Rather, I saw someone who was kind enough to help me.

Wally and I descended into the basement. He asked his girlfriend, a young woman who had named herself after a deity, to help us. So she came down, too. With boxes piled everywhere, the task seemed formidable as we all plunged in. Wally went back outside and returned with Eddy, who had originally boxed my art. A half-hour later, Eddy found my mandalas.

Even though I was happy, I also felt some fear. Were they damaged? The box was dry. There was no sign of mildew. Relief. The drama was finally over.

Wally was happy, too. "Hey, girl. I told you we'd find it."

I gave him a hug and thanked them all.

Eddy carried the heavy box up to my car. On the way home I kept looking over at all the brilliant, splashing rainbows of color in the box. I even reached over and petted them. They were so beautiful. My babies were safe and sound.

I thought about all the lessons I had learned from this experience. When I had felt like a victim, I didn't get the support and help I needed. However, when I let go of the need to have them know how hurt I felt, and focused on being thankful for their kindness, my mandalas were found.

Feeling sincere appreciation and gratitude had changed my focus, which in turn, put me back in my heart. Until I had released the anger, nothing changed. As soon as I was able to feel loving again, my artwork had been found.

When I reached home, I carefully removed the mandalas from the box one at a time, checking for signs of damage. One weaving was stained on the back side, and two other pieces, which had been slightly damaged, were fixable.

This time, I heard a new mantra: "I feel peace in my heart."

Free your heart to feel again. You can make it happen.

~~~ Steps to Happiness NOW! ~~~

69) To be a doormat or not to be a doormat?

Experiences beyond our control may leave us feeling like victims until we can take some form of action from a calm, clear center. By taking positive action in our lives, our attitudes shift, and we can give up the victim stance. When we no longer feel like victims, our difficult scenarios will usually change as well.

70) Put down the megaphone—you don't have to teach anyone else a lesson

Each person is on her own rightful path, although it may not always look that way. I don't know what you need to learn and you don't know what I need to learn. We each get the lessons we need in our own right time. Let go of the need to convert anybody to your way of thinking. Let each person be just as she is.

71) See y'around, Charlie

Guess what? Everyone dies. One day all the people who hurt you will be gone and so will you. Do you want to leave angry energy hanging around for another lifetime? Can you do something about it today?

72) This day is unfolding as it needs to

Answers come—they always do. However, they don't always show up the second you want them. Each day will bring you a special gift if you stay open to receive it. Stay in the flow of what happens today. There is a plan for this day. Your answer will come at its proper time.

Am I Poor, or Is This God's Way of Saying It's Okay for Me to Eat Cat Food?

It's Story Time...

Have you noticed the abundance of pop psychology books which proclaim in one way or another, that if you do what you love, the Universe will pour golden shekels down from the heavens upon your being?

Either those books are right and these authors are deservedly experiencing this flowing of golden shekels upon their beings, or those overly enthusiastic, motivated, you-can-do-it-too-types are wrong. In which case they're still getting their golden shekels, so they're happy either way.

I wanted to find out for myself whether or not their theories held water, or better yet, would allow me to swim. If I did what I loved, would the Universe rise up to support me?

My book was my constant priority. I'd been working on it with a steady sense of commitment and determination. I valued my time writing more than anything else, and I was intent on getting it published. Every word had been written in joy. In other words, I was taking the risk: I was doing what I loved and hoping the Universe would rise up to support me.

At some point, however, my parent's well-meaning inquiries into my financial well-being were beginning to mirror my own increasing concerns. Besides, I'd noticed that none of these wonderful books on prosperity actually gave a time frame in which my miracle was supposed to occur.

I believed that finishing my book was exactly what I needed to be doing. If I took on a full-time job, I knew I wouldn't have the focus of attention I needed in order to complete it. "So God," I ask, "Could I have an advance on some of those golden shekels?"

Watching my bank balance dip uncomfortably low, in spite of all my best intentions, I fell into a state of panic. Should I take some "taxi" job, the kind of job which pays the bills but doesn't nourish the soul? Or should I continue my book in peace, without interruption?

I had to do something. As much as I wanted to save humanity, by this point I couldn't even afford a toaster oven. Although I was trying not to let myself be overwhelmed by fear, I felt a total lack of abundance. So, coming from a sense of lack, I grabbed the first thing that came along—a database entry job for low pay.

Not only was I quickly working too hard for too little, within a few hours I could feel carpal tunnel syndrome kicking in. The whole time I typed, I felt resentful. I couldn't believe this was the best I could find or the best the Universe would provide.

With no other source of income than this dinky, database entry job I despised, I decided to take a risk and let it go in the hopes that I'd immediately find something better. Even though I found someone to replace me at this nightmare job, the woman who had hired me was still resentful I had quit. We blew up at each other. When the smoke wafted away, we were eventually able to talk things through and clear the air.

Since the day was sunny and beautiful, I decided to get in my car and head down the freeway, not quite sure of my final destination. A couple of favorite places came to mind. One was the horse barn overlooking a long hiking trail down to the ocean. As I thought about going there, I felt depressed. Another was the dog park, which also had trails plus lots of nice doggies. When I thought about going there, I felt neutral. Then I thought about heading over to Sausalito and felt happy.

I wanted to be by the water, but didn't know of any place in Sausalito where I could be by the water and not be surrounded by scads of tourists. As I drove down the main road, however, I discovered a beautiful park I'd never noticed before. It was right on the bay. Within two seconds, a frisky Irish setter with a tennis ball in its mouth came bounding over to play.

For the next hour I played with the dog, then lay quietly in lush, beautiful grass under a gorgeous willow tree. The dog, the quiet, and the beauty fed my soul. Feeling recharged, I left the park and decided to stop in and say "hello" to my old coworkers at the magazine I used to run. It was not too far away, and I hadn't been there in ages.

As soon as I walked through the door, the new publisher asked me if I'd help with an article she had been struggling to complete. It took a few hours to finish and she paid me well. This gave me a sense of hope that more opportunities would quickly come along.

That night, with outstretched arms, I said a prayer. "Okay God, I'm open to receive more. Easier. Happier. Better. I give up the struggle." My faith remained unwavering. I would allow money to flow to me from even more unknown sources.

The next day a phone call came out of the blue from a woman I'd met a few years ago. She wanted to hire me to do some writing for an upcoming festival. The job was only for a three-month period. The pay, however, was five times the amount of what I'd just given up. This would cover me for the next three months!

Let go of struggle. It only hurts the muscles in your brain.

~~~ Steps to Happiness NOW! ~~~

73) Thought + emotion + action = creation

When our thoughts are fueled by emotion, whatever we're thinking is most likely going to happen. The catch is, thoughts fueled by fear or any other negative emotion are just as likely to manifest as thoughts fueled by a positive emotion. Whether positive or negative, the stronger the emotion, the more likely it is that the thought will manifest. So think good thoughts!

74) Disarm the resentment time bomb

When something is seeded in resentment, the end result is always more resentment. When resentment is felt and not expressed right from the start, at some point an emotional explosion will occur between both parties. If you feel a sense of resentment forming, as soon as you can, speak up about it. See if you can disarm this time bomb before it explodes between yourself and another.

75) Where does the finger of resentment point?

Resentment comes whenever one compromises oneself. Who do you really resent? Yourself: for not being true to yourself in the first place; for not taking risks; for not taking care of yourself; for not being in your power. Although we tend to blame others when we feel resentful, we are ultimately angry at ourselves.

76) Look for evidence of abundance

Since abundant thinking produces more abundance, and whatever we give our attention to grows, choose to give your attention to the abundance you already have, regardless of what your bank balance shows. Thoughts of lack only produce more lack. As we keep collecting evidence of abundance in any wonderful way it appears in our lives, our fear-based thoughts leave and abundance multiplies.

You Can't Make a Turkey Out of Me

It's Story Time...

As I continued this daily experience of confirming abundance, I waited and watched for it to appear in my life. However, when it didn't appear fast enough according to my way of thinking, I'd find myself in fear. On these days I wouldn't eat enough because I was afraid my money would run out. Interestingly, when I felt money fears and didn't eat enough, no abundance flowed my way. However, on the days when I decided to take care of myself and eat, abundance appeared.

Still, there came a day when my refrigerator reached the point where a box of baking soda stood out as the predominating highlight. I decided, "Enough! I've got to eat. I've got to take care of myself." So off I went to a local health food store and rounded up a little bit of food I considered essential for my well-being, some veggies, some fruit, and some protein.

The turkey burger was on special, so I asked for two pounds, double the amount I'd ever asked for. When I got to the checkout stand, however, I discovered my wallet wasn't in my purse. So I gathered up all the stuff and went to return everything to its proper location throughout the store. However, when I returned the turkey burger to the meat counter, one of the butchers said, "You don't have to return it. We'll loan you the money."

I felt so touched by the gesture, as the butcher turned to his coworker and asked him if he had any change. The coworker reached in his pocket and took out some money.

"Wow, there really are angels in this world. Thank you!"

The butchers started laughing and said they were just joking. They couldn't give me any money.

I'd been suckered. I didn't appreciate having been made the butt of their joke. Still laughing, the butcher said he was sorry. Leaving the store, I felt angry and humiliated, knowing the apology had been anything but sincere.

On the way home, some guy driving by smiled and started to wave at me from his car. Still feeling angry about the incident in the store, I flipped him the bird. The second I did, it occurred to me, he was smiling and waving because he'd seen my "Practice Random Acts of Silliness" bumper sticker on the back of my car. And here I'd just given him the middle finger in response. Poor guy!

As he drove off an exit, I felt terrible. There was no way I could let him know how sorry I felt, except to send him the message psychically, for whatever that was worth. I felt like I'd failed a test. However, now I could totally understand how easily people take their anger out inappropriately on others.

That night, still fuming, I considered my options. I could choose to not shop in that store any more or take some other kind of action. I wrote a letter to the manager.

Within a day, the human resources director called expressing her shock at the behavior of the two employees. The day after that, the manager called also offering his apologies as well. After a nice talk with him, I said, "You know what I'd like as a peace offering? I'd like the two pounds of turkey burger for free." His response was, "Oh, we can do better than that."

Within the week a gift certificate for $25 arrived. That may not sound like a lot of money to you, but at that moment, that money meant a lot to me. It was also the approximate amount I would have spent if I'd been able to buy the food the day I'd forgotten my wallet.

God works in mysterious ways.

~~~ Steps to Happiness NOW! ~~~

77) Go stuff a turkey—make every day Thanksgiving

Since whatever we think multiplies, start appreciating what you already have rather than longing for what you don't. As you keep expressing gratitude, more and more will show up in your life to be grateful for. Notice the good things happening, then put on your Pilgrim suit and give thanks.

78) Abundance begins in your underwear drawer

One way to affirm abundance is to buy yourself all the socks and underwear you need. Any opportunity to replace lack with abundance in one aspect of your life sets the intention that you are open to receive greater abundance in all aspects of your life.

79) Give to yourself

My friend Esha Nagle once said, "Whatever you give to yourself, the Universe will give you more of the same." This applies emotionally, materially, mentally, physically, and spiritually. The more you nurture and nourish any aspect of yourself, the more you will receive. On the other hand, affirm lack or negativity, and that will grow too. So treat yourself really well.

80) Trust in the magic of the universe

If you want something, do not limit the form of how you expect to get it or what it must look like. A costumed man named William Bacon calls himself the "King of Imagination" and strolls through New Age fairs in full festive regalia, granting participants their wishes. He always tells people, "Do not ask for money. Ask for what you would do with the money because this will give the Universe more options in helping you create it."

Psychic Flashes Are Much Better Than Hot Flashes

It's Story Time...

Pretty soon, the baking soda box in the refrigerator had new friends. Tomatoes, tomatillos, zucchini, and fresh basil came from someone's garden. Lemons dropped from a tree in the yard. The out-of-control blackberry bushes in the driveway came into season. A few blocks away, a tree laden with ripe, juicy plums became my main fruit source for the entire summer. I was living off the land, and it was fun.

Although my food needs seemed to be mostly taken care of, I still had no flow of money coming in. Since I didn't think I could make a living by continually getting butchers to insult me, I decided to try a new tactic.

Standing in the middle of my living room one day, I gestured defiantly toward the heavens, and shouted, "I want my Collections Angels, front-and-center right now!" I was adamant. "Now listen to me—I want anything owed to me from anyone in the Universe to come to me right now!" Stamping my foot and shouting into the air, I was undaunted by the neighbors peering in my window wondering if they should get out the big butterfly net.

That afternoon, my phone rang. It was a woman who had owed me money with whom I had not had contact for over a year. After having tried to collect from her many times, I had written it off as a lost cause. This same woman was calling to say she'd left a money order for me in my mailbox because she was too embarrassed to knock on my door and give it to me in person.

That evening, there was a message on my answering machine from another woman who owed me an hour's worth of trade for some work I'd done for her over a year ago. She was offering to give me a bodywork session to complete her end of the trade. Wow! The power of clear intention, insistence, and mighty angels!

Did I know there was such a thing as "Collections Angels?" No, I made it up. The point is, however, it worked. Unknowingly, I had fueled my intention with a magic formula: "Thought + Emotion + Action = Creation."

During this financially difficult period, other miraculous moments happened as well. For example, my naturally curly perm had grown out and my hair had taken on that long, straight, Sixties look. Although I really wanted a perm, I couldn't afford it. I also noticed I was running low on shampoo and dreaded the thought of having to buy a new bottle, because five bucks was a lot right then.

That afternoon there was a message on my answering machine from Oshara. Although we'd been out of touch for a few months and she was living in another state, the message she left on my machine was, "I have a psychic flash you need shampoo. I'm going to send you money so you can buy more shampoo."

When I heard her message, I called her back, telling her how amazing that was because I had just thought about the shampoo that morning. I happened to mention how shaggy I felt because of my worn-out perm.

Her response was, "You need power hair! You can't sign a book contract without power hair! I'm sending you a hundred dollars!"

When I told her my eyes had reddened with little tears in response to her generous offer, she replied, "Oh, come on, Randy, you can do better than that—for a hundred bucks I want wailing!"

There's nothing like a generous friend and a good hair cut to boost one's morale.

~~~ Steps to Happiness NOW! ~~~

81) Turn the abundance valve on

A wonderful teacher of spirituality named Esther Hicks, who channels an entity called "Abraham," (www.hicks-abraham.com) offers the following affirmation: "I can choose what I want based on what I want to experience, rather than on what I think I can or can't afford." Some friends and I pretended we each won ten million dollars. We made lists of how we were going to spend our money. Each of my requests began with, "Randy receives," or "Randy gets," rather than, "Randy buys," in order to increase the likelihood of these things actually happening.

82) Man plans and God laughs (an old Yiddish saying)

God's sense of timing and our sense of timing are not always one and the same. If there's a difference, guess who's gonna win? The quickest way to stifle a miracle is to try to force an outcome. We can block our own good by thinking something needs to look a certain way or happen in a certain way. It usually doesn't. Not being attached to the outcome will keep the flow happening.

83) Everyone walks through molasses

The truth is, I've never met anybody on the way to a miracle who has not encountered feeling stuck. When I've felt stuck, I've also treated myself to some very big doses of hopelessness and despair to accompany it. Feeling stuck is such a crappy feeling. It always feels as though it will last forever. Somehow, it's all part of the plan. If nothing else, feeling stuck helps us build our endurance muscles.

84) Weight=wait

Whatever is weighing us down, i.e., things we're not letting go of, or are still holding on to, will keep us waiting for our Highest Good to emerge. Shift that weight and wait no longer!

Practice Random Acts of Chutzpah

It's Story Time...

Money trickled in like an intravenous drip. I knew I had to somehow create a better financial flow. For the most part, I was feeling stuck and depressed. All I had ever wanted was to get my book published. This was what I'd been working toward and dreaming of. However, in spite of all the steps I'd taken, I had not yet attracted a publisher.

One day I heard a little thought in my head. It was a wild idea, the kind that only a super Eepster would be capable of carrying out. It was way too outrageous, even for an Eepster like me. There was no way I could bring myself to do what I was thinking.

Over the next few months, every time I recalled this wild idea, it made me smile. Finally, I decided I had to act upon it. I was feeling totally stuck. I had nothing to lose, so why not do it?

On a Wednesday afternoon, during the height of rush-hour traffic in the Bay Area, I stood on a meridian at one of the busiest intersections right off of the freeway. I wore heels, my best dress, my new perm, make-up, and a giant cardboard sign:

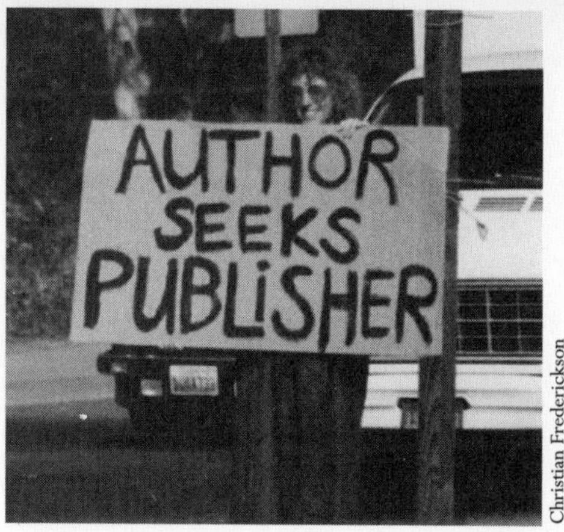

Christian Frederickson

Performing a random act of chutzpah

At first I was literally shaking in my shoes. The response I received, however, was overwhelmingly positive. Pretty soon, I was grinning larger than the hookah-smoking Cheshire Cat. Drivers cheered me on, smiled and waved, gave me the thumbs-up sign, and shouted, "I hope you get it!" and "Good Luck!" from their cars.

And a publisher stopped and gave me his card. It turned out he wasn't interested after all, and that was okay. I didn't really think he was the right one anyway. I filed his rejection slip in my "Stood Up At The Altar" file and moved on.

A funny thing did occur that day, though. Notice my sign read, "Author Seeks Publisher." It didn't read, "Author Seeks Publisher for Book." That same evening a publisher called, not in regards to my book, but to offer me a job as the editor of his magazine. I'd applied for the position the previous week, but when I hadn't heard back from him, I'd thought they'd found someone else, so I'd let it go.

Even though I needed the money, I really didn't want to take this job. I didn't want to compromise my truth, which was that my book was what I was working toward, not a job as an editor of a magazine. So I turned it down.

Then much to my surprise, the publisher made me another offer. He asked if I'd be willing to work the job temporarily, for three to six months, until he found the right person. This time, I accepted. For one, I really needed the money. And secondly, it occurred to me that perhaps I could make a connection for my book by working at this magazine that I couldn't make by sitting in my living room.

Be careful what you ask for, you just might get it!

~~~ Steps to Happiness NOW! ~~~

85) Unstick stuck

Feeling stuck is actually an invitation from your soul to stop everything you're doing, and to listen to those voices in your head which you haven't been paying enough attention to. (No, not those voices, the other voices.) Some call this "listening to your intuition." This is the path of absolute stillness. It requires going inward and tuning into yourself in a different way than you usually do.

86) Follow the forward thread

When you feel stuck, repeatedly ask yourself the wonderful question, "What's the most loving thing I can do for me right now?" Find something which brings you joy—a hobby, animals, anything. Once you discover the most positive thread in your life, keep following it. It will lead you, no matter how trivial or disconnected it seems at the moment, to your ultimate goal. Trust that there is a purpose to all of this and that your rightful place in the universe will be revealed.

87) Shake a leg

When we feel stuck, it feels like any form of forward movement in our lives has screeched to a dead halt. The very act of creating physical movement in our bodies through dance, walking, or anything that physically gets our energy moving, will also help us unstick stuck.

88) Take the biggest risk of all

Sometimes we need to row vigorously and other times we get carried merrily, merrily down the stream. When we're being carried down the stream, our lives seem to flow so easily. When our lives aren't flowing so easily, sometimes taking a baby step or a major risk will help us to unstick stuck.

If You Hate Someone, Imagine He or She Is an Angel

It's Story Time...

This magazine was the first "real job" I'd worked in about a year and a half. The office was a little over an hour from my home which meant a tiresome commute. I soon started to use the drive as my daily God time. I'd talk to God, put in special requests, pray for others and sing. Then the drive actually became something I looked forward to.

On my very first day, the woman I was replacing met with me and within the first two hours proceeded to download everything she'd learned in the last four years.

After that, any questions I asked her were immediately answered with, "I already told you that, and I'm not going to repeat myself," or other similarly obnoxious comments. She reminded me of what my friend Debi calls, "a little petty tyrant." Over the next few weeks, she bombarded me with unwarranted criticisms and judgments of my abilities. I felt stressed and miserable. What had I gotten myself into here?

I started to meet others in this rather large company. Quickly, I learned I was only one among many whom this woman picked apart. In the past, I might have crumbled under the reign of a "little petty tyrant." Now, something inside of me was very different. I would not tolerate this kind of treatment by her or by anyone.

At the same time, I noticed that, little by little, the hearts found me. The people who appeared to be the sweetest in the company sought me out. I was thankful for this small miracle amidst the stress of this new reality.

One night, I shared the difficulties I had been enduring on the job in a group at the Center for Attitudinal Healing. A woman named Mary Kelly said when someone in her life was hard to deal with, she imagined that she or he was an angel. Every time she had done this, the situation had changed for the better.

As I tried to imagine this woman at work as an angel, I immediately saw her with a little, curlicue piggy tail and tiny angel wings. Obviously, she was a piggy angel. Not wanting to put someone down, and the image of a piggy angel not being very flattering, I thought, "Okay, if she's a piggy angel, what am I?"

Immediately, I received the image of a braying jackass. "Hee-haw!" I thought. "A jackass is stubborn, persevering, and can't be budged. A stubborn, persevering jackass can hold its own against a piggy angel any old day." The image of "piggy angel and jackass" made me smile and dig my heels in deeper.

After that, whenever we butted heads at work, which was frequently, I imagined "piggy angel and jackass" going at it and stood my ground. I also thought of the quote from *A Course In Miracles*, "I can choose peace instead of this," and endeavored to do just that each time there was a flare-up.

When piggy angel told me she didn't feel I could do the job and believed the magazine would fall apart because of me, I empathetically encouraged her to talk to the publisher and express her concerns. When she told me she had already done so, I didn't go rushing off to defend myself. Why should I? I was secure in who I was and in my skills. I thought of another line from *A Course In Miracles*, "In my defenselessness my safety lies." I had no need to defend myself; I just needed to do my job. So I told piggy angel to relax. Now that the publishers knew exactly how she felt, she didn't need to keep this weight on her shoulders. Still, piggy angel was relentless.

I needed to constantly keep myself centered in order to shield myself from her endless barrage of mean-spiritedness. Each day on my drive to work, I would set up my day. I'd decide what kind of day I wanted to have, and then I would ask God to help bring me that kind of day. For example, I'd ask for a day of ease, or a day filled with surprises, or a day of happiness, or a day in which I could work undisturbed. I noticed that whatever I asked for, my day would unfold with those particular qualities. By setting up my day first, I was less susceptible to piggy angel's comments because I'd already programmed my day in a different way.

Not only did I dress exceptionally well during this time period, I smiled, laughed, and brought a feeling of positive energy and joy into the workplace. I held my head up high and was friendly. I wanted to radiate happiness instead of stress. And for my coworkers I also wanted to rebuild a sense of team spirit, which had long since been squelched by the piggy angel.

Every day, one of my prayers on my way to work was, "God, use me as You will." By focusing on what I could give rather than on what was in it for me, I stayed in that place of love, rather than collapsing from fear of the piggy angel's continual bombardment.

Since my self-esteem was high, the piggy angel no longer represented a threat. One day, piggy angel left a message marked, "Urgent" on my voice mail. She wanted an unrealistic number of articles completed that day. We spoke on the phone and immediately started doing battle. I told her I would no longer tolerate being spoken to in a condescending or critical manner.

I further continued, "And by the way, you sent me a message coded, 'Urgent' on my voice mail." I raised my voice dramatically. "Appendicitis is urgent! Page 56 is *not* urgent!"

She started to speak, "How can I *stress* to you..."

I interrupted, "That's the problem. There's too much *stress* around here and nobody's having fun! There's no reason why this shouldn't be fun." She backed off, stymied. I'd won that round.

That night I called her. It hadn't been my intention to "win." It was my intention for us to work together in harmony until her departure a month later, and to bring our dynamic to neutral if at all possible. We talked civilly and she came up with a solution that worked for both of us. I would return to her any assignment she'd given to me, no matter at what stage of completion. She would finish them without me, and I would start working on what would be my first issue, which was three months away.

This was a solution we both could live with. After that, there was no problem between us, perhaps because there was little need for us to interact. The best thing about this agreement though, was I felt as though I'd handled this situation in a healthy, positive way. I didn't let myself get plowed over. The threat, the dynamic, the power struggle—all of it—went poof! I'd passed the test. There were no more problems between the piggy angel and the jackass after that. The stress left. We were equals in this game, and life at work improved.

Claim your power.

~~~ Steps to Happiness NOW! ~~~

89) Pray for the magical unfolding of your day

Set up your day with a prayer just before you pull into work each morning. Bless the day ahead of you, asking it be filled with pleasant surprises or opportunities to grow. Also use this time to bless difficult people so they will experience something wonderful in their day too. This routine will always make your day feel better.

90) Wear the attitude

If someone is giving you a hard time, you might choose to see it as an opportunity to overcome the victim stance. Do whatever it takes to increase your sense of self-esteem. Dress to the nines. Smile. Hold your head up high. Radiate positive energy. Ask to be guided to your Highest Good in every second.

91) Intimidation is an agreement

Intimidation requires both an intimidator and an intimidatee. Both come from fear. The intimidator is a bully who is afraid of losing control. The intimidatee, on the other hand, allows him- or herself to be intimidated. The intimidatee is always fearful about whatever the intimidator will dole out next. The way to break this agreement is for the intimidatee to step beyond her fear by either speaking up for herself or by walking away.

92) Make God the CEO of your life

Jobs come and go—even for people with matching dishes. If your job suddenly disappears, stop and breathe. Your life is not about a particular company. It is about working on behalf of others, in service to society, the planet, animals, the environment, wherever it is you feel called to serve. If you hold in your heart that you work for God, Love, or for the Highest Good of all, you will continually be lead along your rightful path. However, you may still need to kick out more resumes.

SECTION 3

UNDER THE MICROSCOPE

Family Up Close (and a Few Furry Friends)

- Our ability to allow ourselves to feel happy is largely connected to our relationship with our family of origin. In this section, we're going to examine our roots—not the chestnut-brown ones with platinum-blonde frizzy ends—but our biological roots.

- Whether crappy or happy, by examining the dynamics of our families, we acknowledge the richness of personal connection. Who we are is a result of who we've been, who we've loved, and who has loved (or not loved) us back. It is also a result of all the choices we've made along the way, including our willingness to communicate and our desire to heal with others.

- We will further look at how important animals can be in the process of healing or opening our hearts. Whether human or animal, we can discover a truer reflection of who we are and what we value through the eyes of those whom we love.

Who Is She Really?

It's Story Time...

I'm having an identity crisis. Do you know who I am?

If you are my father, you call me Renae (your sister's name). If you are my mother, you call me Shirley (also your sister's name). If you are my brother, you call me Roxane (your wife's name).

Did you ever have this kind of problem where no one gets your name right—not even your own parents?

Sometimes my father's thoughts race ahead of his speech. One time he called me "Rabby." What he meant to say was, "Randy, the rabbi..." My father has also accidentally called me Ranchy, Raunchy, and Rather.

Rather, Dad? Rather? This is someone who needs special tutoring to get his daughter's name right. I've got the solution! Family Flash Cards.

I tried it at a family gathering. I wrote my name on a full-sized sheet of notebook paper, stapled a piece of yarn at the top corners, and wore it around my neck. This elegant addition to my attire did not go unnoticed. My parents got my name right all evening. So did everyone else. You see, a little visual reminder goes a long way.

One of the problems in my family is that we are overrun with names beginning with "R." There is a Rachel, a Renae, a Roxane, a RoseAnn, and a Randy—me. The odds of someone calling one of us by the wrong name automatically runs high. By using Family Flash Cards, no one ever need make a mistake again.

One problem solved, but wait, there are biggies ahead. If my own parents can't call me by the right name without flash cards, can you imagine what the rest of the world is doing to it? Actually you don't have to imagine. I will tell you. For ten years I've kept a notebook filled with all the other names people have called me.

My own bank sent me checks with the name *Randy Peyper* printed on them. I've also collected airline tickets, hotel reservations, insurance statements, employee memos, and bunches of other letters that show a different name, gender, or marital status for me. I now have sixty-nine entries in my collection.

PHONETIC ATTEMPTS—THE "GOOD TRY" CATEGORY

Randy Peysir
Randi Pieser
Randy Pizer
Randy Pizor
Randy Pyser
Randy Pyzer
Randy Peiser
Randie Peyser
Randee Peyser

HERBS & SPICE SELECTION

Randy Pepper

OUR FRIEND FROM THE BIRD KINGDOM

Randy Peeper

SPEECH IMPEDIMENT CATEGORY

Randy Peither

Randy Pyther

MARRIED AND MALE

Mr. Randy Reyser

Ron Peyser

Mr. Randy Puiser

Mr. Randy Ruth Peyser

Mr. and Mrs. Randy Peyser

Mr. and Mrs. Reyser

Mr. Randy Peyser—almost a daily occurrence in my mailbox

When I was graduating from high school I received advertisements from various branches of the Armed Forces looking for young male recruits. When the Marines sent a letter to Mr. Randy Peyser saying they were looking for a few good men, I wrote them back saying, "So am I."

FOREIGN ENTRIES

Rendi

Ranndi

NAME I NEVER WANT TO BE CALLED AGAIN

Mr. Randy Peuper

NAMES I CAN'T PRONOUNCE

Randy Piuser

Randy Pfiser

Randy Peiyser

Randy Peyeser

Randy Peysyser

WHO COULD THEY POSSIBLY MEAN?

Raydy Peyser
Raney Peyser
Ranoy Peyser
Randay Peyser
Randey Peyser

TWO WRONG TURNS

Sandy Peyson
Ranoy Peusar
Randi Peysner
Randi Pacer
Randi Peysor
Randi Visor

OUT ON ALL THREE COUNTS

Mr. Randi Reyer

SO CLOSE, YET SO FAR

Randy Peter
Randy Pelzer
Randy Pevser
Randy Payser
Randy Paisner
Randy Reiser
Randy Reyser
Randy Renser
Randy Peyer
Randy Peyper
Randy Peysen
Randy Peyson
Randy Payson
Randy Peyset
Randy Peysev
Randy Byser
Randy Feyser
Randy Teyser
Randy Deyser
Randy Plyser
Randy Leyser
Randy Kaiser
Randy Peifer
Randy Peyfer
Randy Peiper
Randy Peysler
Randy Peyster
Randy Peysey
Sandy Peyser

So, who am I really? *Randy Peyser.* It says so on the cover. See? Easy.

Okay, class, let's practice what we've learned. Let's conjugate this together. Repeat after me, "I am who I am. You are who you are. We are who we are. They are who they are." Those other names are somebody else.

Actually, there are some other names I do like. These are the names from people I love.

NAMES MY FRIENDS CALL ME

Randessa—I turned all my friends into royalty for a "royal tea" party. I was Princessa Randessa. The Randessa part stuck.

Randessa Lily—an extension of Princessa Randessa.

Randessa La Kookenaya or La Kook!—Scrabble playing holy name.

Peezer—childhood name given to me by my friend Linda when we were twelve years old. Reserved for her use only.

Raggamandy—name given to me by a two-year-old who couldn't say "Randy."

Randelia Bedelia and Pandy Reyser—names my friend Judy calls me.

Randers—must be my little Dutch girl name.

Auntie Randy—wow, I'm old enough to be an aunt.

Chicky or Dolly—what my mother calls me.

Randalah—my grandma's special name for me.

Eepster—name I call myself.

ANSWERS TO QUESTIONS ASKED ABOUT THE NAME "RANDY"

No, it's not short for anything.
Yes, it's my real name.
No, my parents didn't want a boy.
Yes, I know what it means in England.

Walking the Gender Tightrope

I like my name a lot. I always thought I'd be a different person if my name was spelled Randi with an "i," the typical feminine version, rather than Randy with a "y." But that wouldn't be me. I am who I am and I spell me the way I spell me.

I like having a traditionally male name and also being a very feminine person. I think I'm more evenly gender-balanced as a result of my name—as long as I don't have to lift anything. I hate to lift things. Please remember that. Don't ever ask me to lift things. When you move, I'll come and pack the dishware, just don't ask me to lift things, okay?

I've noticed I'm not the only gender tightrope walker these days. Gender balancing is becoming much more common. My women friends tell me how they are balancing their inner male side with their female side. My men friends talk about how they're integrating their inner female side with their male side. Sometimes it gets confusing to figure out who's on which side anymore.

I know what would help—a role model. Someone who knows how to very clearly and distinctly balance their inner male with their inner female and vice versa.

I could be the role model. Pick me! Pick me! Please! Please! Goody. Thanks!

RANDY S FEMALE SIDE vs. RANDY S MALE SIDE

RANDY S FEMALE SIDE	RANDY S MALE SIDE
Prays	Negotiates
Creates	Takes care of details
Writes books	Gets them published
Cooks	Takes out garbage
Feels feelings	Thinks about stuff
Loves to stay at home	Loves to be out in the world
Is soft, gentle, and nurturing	Is powerful and intense
Plays angelic harp & guitar	Plays pounding rock drums
Has Daddy do her taxes	Spends refund

There! Am I a great role model or what? My list proves it—I am perfectly and completely balanced across the gender line.

Now, Do I Sit Down to Pee —Or Do I Stand Up?—

When I was in college, my father was grasping the early concepts of feminism. He quickly learned to say that he had two kids, "a boy and a woman." Not only was he correct about my gender, he also knew the appropriate terminology to make me happy. Dad's an adult. He understands these things.

Little kids on the other hand are having the darndest time trying to figure out what I am. And this seems to be important to them.

You know how little kids will say whatever is on their minds? I've often been asked point-blank by little kids who don't know me, "Are you a boy or a girl?" Of course, sometimes I've wanted to ask that of people I've seen on the street too, so I can understand the kids' curiosity. Even so, it still surprises me each time I hear it.

One time I was in a Laundromat drumming when this little kid walked in. He was about four or five. He watched with total attention as I played. When I stopped, the first thing he said was, "Are you a guy or a woman?" I told him I was a woman. His response was, "Oh." Then he pointed to the drum. "Can I try it?" Once gender was established, he was ready to play.

Another time I was in the library checking out some books. I got the same kind of question from some other little kid I'd never seen before. "Are you a girl or a boy?"

What is it about me that kids can't figure out? All my friends tell me I am very feminine. What's so confusing?

I know what it is. They must have seen my birth certificate. That must be it. On my birth certificate, "Male" is typed in the box marked "Sex." It's crossed out and "Female" is scrawled in below it. Maybe all the kids secretly know this and they want to know the truth. Do I sit down to pee or do I stand up? Am I a boy or a girl?

What I want to know is, why didn't they just give me a new birth certificate without a glaring mistake on it? This is my first legal document, the one which tells the whole world who I am. My entire life, I only have one official birth certificate, and it has a big boo-boo on it. Even if I request copies of it, the boo-boo is still there.

Would you want to have a big boo-boo on your birth certificate? I don't think so. Now, look what's happened. There's all these kids who can't figure out my gender.

So far, I've only found one kid who has some clarity on the subject. I was sitting in a Wendy's restaurant when this little girl pointed to me and said to her mother, "Mommy, that's a lady."

Yes, she got it right! The fries are on me.

~~~ Steps to Happiness NOW! ~~~

93) Claim your name

There are nicknames that feel loving and others that put you down. Never allow anyone to call you "New Age Flake," "dumb-dumb," or any other word that doesn't make you feel proud of who you are. Your name is your calling card in the Universe. You deserve to be called by the name that makes you feel your best.

94) Marvel at the miracle that you are

How did you get here anyway? Technically speaking you are one in a million—in terms of sperm, that is. Isn't that miraculous? Somehow you wound up in a body with all sorts of nifty parts. It's all pretty amazing if you stop to think about it. Stop to think about it.

95) Carry a winning attitude. Put it in your briefcase and just be yourself

Remember the wisdom of that famous sage, Popeye, "I yam what I yam"? Yes, you are who you are and who you are is enough. You deserve love and all good things just because you are you. Look in the mirror at the most special being in the world—YOU—and say, "Hi, wonderful You. Thanks for existing." Go do it now while I'm still watching.

96) Express your male and female sides

Many women are becoming stronger, while many men are becoming softer (in a metaphorical sense, that is). I attended a meeting where all the men were expressing deep feelings. At the same time, all the women were focused on taking action. We'd unknowingly reversed the stereotypical roles where men "do" and women "feel." Take note of the different male and female aspects of your personality.

Why Barbie's Boobs Are Gold

It's Story Time...

As kids, my brother Ted and I fought constantly. We fought over who Mom loved best. (I don't know why, but neither of us seemed to care if Dad had a favorite.) Ted and I agreed on one thing, though. We both thought Mom loved me best. And this made him furious—furious enough to get back at me by painting the boobs on all of my Barbies with gold, car model paint. My mother said she loved us both equally and always had. We never believed her.

Ted continued to bug me all the time. I had really long legs, kind of like a stick figure, so he started calling me, "Pants."

"Hey, Pants! Hey, Randy Pants!"

He got all the kids in the neighborhood to say it. "Hi, Randy Pants."

"Mom! Make him stop! He's calling me Pants again!" I endlessly wailed in sorrow. It made no difference. He was relentless.

When I was seven, my mom took me to play therapy. It was all my brother's fault. Everything which had ever happened to me in my entire life and all my past lives was a result of the low self-esteem I had developed as a direct result of him calling me "Randy Pants."

There. How do you feel now, Ted? Guilty? Good. It's all your fault. Everything that has ever happened to me and every reason why my life has not been picture-perfect is your fault.

Even the readers agree with me. What do you mean you're reading this and you don't agree with me? Take my side. *My* side. You always take his side. No fair!

Okay, so it's not his fault. Still, it felt good to blame him. I always wanted to.

The truth is that second grade was just too much for me. I couldn't cope with the stress of the school curriculum. The school was trying an experiment. Actually, the school didn't try anything, because the school is just a building. The grownups inside the school were trying the experiment. They asked a question amongst themselves, "What if we make all the kids work two years or more beyond their grade level?"

When I was in second grade, one of my spelling words was "conflagration." Well there's a word that comes up every day in conversation. Wasn't that important to learn in second grade?

That gives you an idea of what school was like. The end result was a bunch of kids accomplishing work way beyond their grade level, and lining up at the water fountain every day to take their tranquilizers.

My mother told me that once during a therapy session, I was playing with the dolls and I said to my therapist, "Here's the mommy doll, and here's the daddy doll, and here's me, and here's the baby doll. Wait. There's too many dolls. We don't need all these dolls. Let's bury the baby doll in the sandbox." Bye-bye, Ted. (Smirk.)

Wait. What's this? Move over, Randy. Move over, Ted. The debate over who Mom likes best has been settled once and for all. I have been dethroned.

Now there are grandchildren. (And if there had been a debate over who Dad liked best, that would be settled too. Dad could single-handedly fund a yearly salary for one employee at Toys 'R' Us with all the money he spends on gifts for those kids.)

The kids are Ted's. I've thought about having children and have decided I'd rather be a mentor then a "tor" mentor. All my friends think I'd be a great parent. I used to think that too. Then I spent a week at my brother's house and now I think I'd be the mom from hell. Whoops. We don't swear in front of the children. I'd be the mom from heck. There. That's better.

The kids challenged all of my kid-raising fantasies. For instance, I always thought if I had kids, I wouldn't have a TV in the house. Wrong. After two days of three kids fighting, not having one second of time to myself, nor being able to have a conversation with another adult without being interrupted to referee or watch something, I have become a firm believer in the almighty, all-powerful, baby-sitting television set.

Ted, on the other hand, is a good parent, and so is his wife, Roxane. They set limits on the amount of TV-watching, and they're doing a great job raising those kids.

There, Ted. I said it in print. Now pay me! No, I meant every word of it. There is no agreement for them to pay me for saying they are model parents. I just made it up. However, it is true. The part about them being good parents, I mean.

Meanwhile, the four-year-old, who has just discovered his genitals, is in the bathtub singing, "Happy Birthday, Dear Peenie" to himself. Last week he drew caterpillars with crayons all over the walls of his room. Pretty soon he's going to find the gold paint and go after his sisters' Barbies.

Ha-ha, Ted. Another cycle begins.

Look forward to what comes next.

~~~ Steps to Happiness NOW! ~~~

97) Stand out in a crowd

I have a friend who had just gotten a hot-shot job in a Fortune 500 company. One weekend, he brought his kids in to see where their daddy worked. While in the elevator, the general counsel for the entire corporation got on, whereupon my friend's daughter, aged three, grabbed the guy's pants leg and announced, "My daddy air-poops." When nobody said anything, she pulled his pants again and said it louder. The general counsel always recognized my friend after that.

98) If you can't say it with flowers, at least say it without getting in trouble

My brother's kids are not allowed to swear or name-call. During a fight, his seven-year-old shouted to her sister, "You're every bad name in the whole world." I'd say she handled that rather well; she expressed her rage and didn't wind up in Time-out. Can you do the same?

99) Remember your childhood innocence

When I was twelve, I totally believed my best friend when she told me she buttered her mom's kitchen sink to keep the ants from coming up the drain. Then much to her delight, we went to my house so I could ask my mother how come we didn't do that. After looking at me like I was nuts, Mom and my friend had a great laugh. Appreciate the precious innocence of a child.

100) Gather that which is dearest to your heart

A group of elderly women created an improvisational dance based on the open-ended theme of gathering something. Afterwards, they shared what they had just been pretending to pick. One picked flowers, and another, ripe, juicy fruits. Then one woman said, "I was gathering children." As she danced off, I noticed she seemed the happiest of all.

We're Not the Waltons—
We're the Peysers!

It's Story Time...

In the following scene, can you detect the one detail which is true?

> Crickets chirped in the background as the last light was dimmed. Wishing each other a good night's sleep, we each drifted off into a cozy state of slumber.
>
> "Goodnight, Randy-Girl."
>
> "Goodnight, Momma."
>
> "Goodnight, Ted-boy."
>
> "Goodnight, Daddy."

Could you guess which statement was true? Clue: It involved bugs. Yes, the crickets chirped. However, the last light was never dimmed because someone had invariably forgotten to turn it off.

Nighttime was not the time for cozy slumber, either. It was the war zone—the time when Mom and Dad screamed at each other so much I thought they'd take the paint off the walls. I don't think anybody ever got a good night's sleep in my house, except perhaps for the gerbils and the fish.

As for me, I grew up in a state of perpetual fear. Would Mommy leave Daddy? Would Daddy leave Mommy? Was it my fault? Was it Ted's fault? What could I do to make them love each other? What could I do to get them to stop screaming and fighting?

It may come as no surprise, that I, as a kid, could do nothing to alleviate the tension in my family. By the time I was in my teens, I repeatedly fantasized about driving the family car over a cliff. Instead of saying "bye-bye" to this cold, cruel world, however, I lay in my bed and cried for hours on end.

No one, including me, had a clue as to why I was so depressed. We were, after all, a normal family, just like *your* family when *you* were growing up. Isn't this the way all families (dys)functioned?

My parents decided they'd better send me to a psychiatrist. Little did they know, the doc was an alcoholic who had more problems than I did. I decided to change therapists.

At the time, my mother was volunteering for the local crisis line (as if all the crises in our own family weren't enough), and she referred me to a nearby agency where I arranged for an initial interview.

The therapist seemed nice enough. "So, how are things at home?"

It sounded like an innocent question. "Fine, fine. Just fine. No problem. Everything's hunky-dory."

I truly believed this. I had no idea anything was wrong with the way we interacted as a family. The therapist said he would like to meet with my family anyway.

Mom and Dad agreed to go—not because there was anything wrong with them, but because I was the one who was severely depressed, and they would do anything to help me.

At first my brother refused because he was sure he was going to be blamed for my problems. (See "Why Barbie's Boobs Are Gold.") But after the first month, he joined us.

The therapist taught us how to communicate better with one another and also how to fight fairly. For example, we learned that when any two members of a family were engaged in a fight or even in a discussion, it was typical for another family member to take sides or be drawn in to take sides. The therapist taught us how to disengage from third-party interference.

We practiced our new skills by having two people in the family engage in a conversation. The other two family members were not allowed to comment or take sides, no matter how hard it was to keep our mouths shut. A conversation or a fight between two family members became just that, an interaction between only those two people.

As a result, whenever my parents fought after that, I no longer felt like I needed to defend one against the other. However they worked out their problems was between the two of them.

My brother and I had our own problems to work out as well. Ted and I didn't talk to each other that much. I was hoping that through the process of therapy, we could establish a stronger brother/sister relationship. One time in a session, I asked him if he would be willing to spend some time with me, to do anything, it didn't matter what. I just wanted us to be closer.

He said, "No."

I couldn't hold back the tears. My mother started crying, too.

Immediately, the therapist intervened. "Mom, why are you crying?"

"Because Ted hurt Randy."

"Mom, while that may appear to be true, Randy's pain and her tears are hers. They're not yours. This didn't happen to you. When you take on someone else's feelings, this is called "fusion." It's important that you let Randy have her own feelings."

The therapist was right. The emotional overlapping between my mother and me, along with our unspoken agreement to not hurt each other, was actually hurting us both even more. I would cry when she cried. She would cry when I cried. I had become afraid to express my feelings—especially anger—because I didn't want to upset her. Instead of expressing and releasing the anger building up inside of me for years, it had imploded in on me in the form of depression.

The therapist helped us to untangle this mess. My feelings became *my* feelings and my mother's feelings became *her* feelings. Slowly I strengthened inside. I learned I was entitled to any and all of my feelings. Interestingly enough, once I started expressing my pent-up anger and began to release it, the feeling of depression, which had lasted for five years, lifted.

Over twenty years later, my family still uses the skills we learned in those six months of therapy. Maybe we are not exactly like the Waltons, but I am glad we are exactly like the Peysers.

Last week a card arrived in the mail from my parents. My mother wrote, "Dearest Randy, I'm so glad you chose us for your parents. You are loved and cherished. You're a gift from God." Dad wrote, "I write the checks. Mom writes the notes." Enclosed was a hundred bucks.

I feel very loved and supported by them. I know that no matter what, they care about me. They always have. Their love for each other has also deepened and grown. The war is finally over.

As for my brother, he still doesn't spend time with me, but hey, that's life.

I am so grateful to that therapist. I wish I could tell him how much all of our lives were affected by his skillful interaction. Thank you, Norman Ritchie. I hope you read this.

And thank you to all of the Norman Ritchies of the world—those angels in human form who come into our lives for a short period of time, and whose impact lasts forever.

Seek out wise counsel. Find a Norman Ritchie.

~~~ Steps to Happiness NOW! ~~~

101) It's okay to fight if you do it right

I grew up in a home where the rule for arguing was, "Whoever's loudest, wins." My whole family is louder than I am, so I had to find other ways to make my point. Once when my father and I had an argument, I regressed back to the Stone Age and threw a plate of lasagna. (I'm not proud.) I don't recommend this, although it did get his attention, and I didn't need to shout.

102) Make peace with your family

I know this is a toughie. However, if you don't make peace, the lasagna's going to stick to the wall forever. Fortunately, my father and I apologized to each other, and I can still eat Italian food in the house. If someone isn't willing to make peace with you, scrape the lasagna off the wall and make peace with yourself.

103) Do not keep claiming the past—be in the Now

It's never too late for hearts to heal. When I was growing up, my parents fought more than all the "Rocky" movies combined. Now, after forty-six years of marriage, they really love each other. They even place little "I LOVE YOU" notes around the house for each other to find. If my parents can work things out, I'm convinced anybody can. Anybody. It may take some doing, however.

104) If you're waiting for happily-ever-after, create it Now

I once asked a woman who had been married for fifty years the secret of the longevity of her marriage. Without missing a beat, the woman replied, "Well, we hold hands a lot to keep from killing each other." You see, everybody finds their own solution. Others may think they have your answer, however, you are the only one who really knows how to create magic in your life.

Bubby Ceile and the Infamous Fruit Cocktail Incident

It's Story Time...

My father's mother didn't want to be thought of as being old enough to be a grandmother when I was born. I guess she thought "bubbies" were younger than "grandmas" because that's what she decided she wanted to be called. Bubby is Yiddish for grandma. So my brother Ted and I grew up calling her Bubby Ceile.

Bubby Ceile supervised the children's playroom at some Jewish resort hotels in New York and New Jersey. This meant whenever we visited her at these hotels, Ted and I got to do cool art projects like making mosaic ashtrays or potholders on those little plastic looms. No one in my family smoked, and I don't ever remember seeing my mom actually use one of those potholders. That's beside the point. It was fun.

Once when I was twelve years old, Bubby Ceile showed me an old browned photograph, and it looked like I was in the picture. I didn't understand how she could have this picture of me, because all the girls in the photo were wearing styles from some long ago time. It turned out it was Bubby Ceile at age twelve. It was really strange to see how we looked so alike.

My grandmother married in her thirties and had two children, my father, Marvin, and then my Aunt Renae. She also raised my father's younger cousin Stan, whose mother had died. Her husband, Theodore, was a burlesque comedian in the

Catskills and was not around very much. He died shortly after World War II.

She never remarried. One time, she told me she had met someone she liked. Then she discovered that he always chewed with his mouth open. That was that.

Bubby Ceile appeared content with her choice to remain single. She certainly stayed busy and I never ever heard her complain about feeling lonely.

Once or twice a year, my family and I would drive to New York, or in her later years, to Miami Beach, to see her. I have many happy memories of our visits. Bubby Ceile would get so excited. She was a great cook and she'd prepare an elaborate dinner with lots of courses, including homemade ice-cream for dessert, and she'd serve us on her fine china. Other relatives, who I normally didn't get to see, would show up too.

Bubby Ceile also had a piano, and I loved to tinkle on it. My father's family was very musical. Everyone could play "Heart and Soul." And each of them did. My father played it. Then my cousin. Then my other cousin. Then my aunt. I hate that song. Doesn't anyone know a different song? Stop already. You already played that one! Play something else. Oh, great. The only other song everyone knows is "Chopsticks." And here it comes.

There was one thing, however, about all the apartment buildings she ever lived in that was worse than a thousand verses of "Heart and Soul" and "Chopsticks." Although Bubby Ceile was meticulously clean, every apartment she rented had roaches.

When we'd drive down to Miami Beach to see her, my father would immediately run to the store and buy a bunch of roach motels, because the roaches really upset him.

My brother and I started making up roach jokes to alleviate Dad's stress. Ted would look in the little roach motel and say something like, "There's two more checked in at the Fountainbleu for the night." Or I'd pipe in with "Buenas noches, little roaches."

For some reason we started calling the roaches "company." I don't even remember how this got started or why. One day, my brother was fixing Bubby Ceile's toaster. He turned it over and company popped out, nicely toasted. Even though we loved Bubby Ceile's cooking, we ate out a lot when we visited her in Miami Beach.

Once a year, Bubby Ceile came to Connecticut to visit us. As soon as her luggage was in the front door, she'd go find the antique Singer sewing machine she stored at our house and start sewing.

Bubby Ceile liked to sew. Actually, that's putting it mildly. For a long time, it seemed as though she lived to sew. Sometimes we'd want to take her out somewhere. She preferred to stay at home and sew for us.

She surprised me with these wonderful pants and vest sets she'd make for me. Unfortunately, the fabrics she used were the "great buys" she found in the worst of thrift stores.

I don't know who invented these fabrics or why. They either came in shades of gray, or they would stain from water, or the threads would disintegrate as I wore the outfit, or they itched badly. I'd go to school and sit down cautiously just in case the outfit was going to fall apart. One time I remember sitting down and hearing the seat of my pants starting to split. I waddled home.

What was worse than all of that was what happened *while* she was sewing. One of the things Bubby Ceile knew how to do was instill fear. And one of the biggest fears she instilled in me was the fear of stepping on a needle. When I was really young she told me, "Randy, never step on a needle. It could travel up your bloodstream and pierce your heart. A pin, okay. You can step on that. A pin has a head, and that won't get under your skin and kill you."

Bubby Ceile was forever dropping pins and needles. One time I reached into the fridge and started to pour an opened container of fruit cocktail into a bowl. There was a needle in the can. I freaked. To this day, I chew all my food exceptionally well and filter all liquids carefully around my tongue—even if it's a clear glass of water—to make sure I'm not swallowing any needles.

The day after the infamous fruit cocktail incident, I was walking barefoot out in the backyard when I spotted another one of her needles in the grass near the picnic table. That was it for walking barefoot. Even now, I rarely walk barefoot and when I do, I walk cautiously, arching my feet to avoid stepping on needles.

Bubby Ceile was a self-proclaimed health nut. She taught me how to grow mung bean sprouts and warned me about the danger of nitrates in hot dogs. She froze things in glass jars and never used aluminum foil, just in case it caused Alzheimer's.

She prided herself on being a good cook and had hundreds of recipes which she stored on little 3x5 index cards in an old shoebox. My parents sent me the shoebox this past summer.

The recipes were divided into typical categories like casseroles, desserts, Passover recipes, and so forth. As I went through the shoebox, I discovered that mixed in with every section of her recipes were recommendations for curing almost every ailment or disease on the face of the Earth and beyond.

This old, musty shoebox represented a lifetime of accumulated tips and household hints she valued. She had collected these recipes for over forty years. What made me chuckle, though, was the order in which she had categorized all of this information. For example, here is a series of index cards in the order in which they lay:

When Cooking a Pot Roast. Add 3 or 4 T. strong black coffee to the gravy. Makes it very tasty.

Hair Treatment. Heat up olive oil or Castor oil. Rub into scalp and on ends of hair. Wrap around with towel.

Roasting Guide for Beef Rib Roast.

Mildew Stains. Soak pieces in buttermilk, moving them around often till liquid reaches all spots. Soak till they disappear then rinse thoroughly in cold water, then wash.

Bedsores (Decubitus Ulcers). A high concentration of sugar applied daily to bedsores under a special airtight bandage clears them up. Honey may also be used.

Refinishing Wood Floors. Remove shellac with denatured alcohol. Just spread alcohol over floor. Give it a second or two and then wipe up the softened shellac with steel wool or a coarse cloth.

No Bake Cheese Cake.

I also found individual index cards with multiple hints on them, the combinations of which were pretty unique. For example:

To Remove Soft Corns or Hard Corns. Soak feet, clean, dry. Use 1/2 fresh lemon, cut side to the corn. Secure with

Saran Wrap, masking tape, and stocking over-nite. In the morning, spread the flesh and the corn pops out. Pepper is a good source of chromium. Avoid bubble baths and douches.

Insomnia. Dilute pineapple juice with water or drink apple juice before retiring.

Cleaning Vinyl Furniture. Shake baking soda on a moistened rough-knit cloth and rub in the vinyl. Wash with mild soap suds. Rinse and wipe dry.

Hemorrhoids. 400mg Vit. E twice daily as a suppository.

Now, about all this advice: If you try the insomnia cure and wind up waking up all night to get up and pee, don't blame me. Or if you want to stick Vitamin E up your "you-know-where" for your hemorrhoids, ask your doctor first. Remember, I'm just sharing tips out of a shoebox.

Bubby Ceile memorized everything she ever read in *Prevention Magazine* and was knowledgeable about all kinds of alternative health issues. When she was in her early fifties, she was diagnosed with breast cancer and had a radical mastectomy. She refused to take painkillers and had a relative sneak in vitamins and bring her the foods she wanted. In four days she was out of the hospital. Her doctor was amazed. She claims it was her diet, her vitamins, and her longtime exercise regime.

Bubby Ceile was an exercise fanatic. She never drove a car, rarely took buses, and walked almost everywhere she needed to go. Even when she grew old, I remember visiting her in her little apartment in Miami Beach, and while my family and I were still trying to sleep, I could hear the pitter-patter of her little feet and her tiny ninety-four-pound body jogging briskly between our cots in the living room.

Every morning around 7:00, she'd be waving her arms up and down, clenching and unclenching her hands. She'd let out a long series of pronounced "ho-ho-ho's" like she was Santa Claus practicing for Christmas. "Laughing is good for the abdominal muscles," she said.

She also did eye exercises that made her look really strange. She'd roll her eyes in all directions and blink a lot. When going through the shoebox, I found her eye exercises, which filled both sides of an index card.

Adelle Davis's book, *Let's Eat Right to Keep Fit,* was Bubby Ceile's bible. I remember Bubby Ceile got really angry at Adelle Davis when she died of cancer. Years later, however, in spite of all the exercise, vitamins, and health foods, Bubby Ceile died of cancer, too.

When Bubby Ceile could no longer care for herself, my father helped her move to a nursing home back in New York.

The home was decorated in a hot pink that didn't know when to quit. There were giant balloons, lighting fixtures, walls, curtains, chairs, and tables—all in this intense, hideous hot pink. Even Mary Kay would have winced.

I was in college at the time and didn't see much of Bubby Ceile then. I would write her and send her happy, colorful magic marker drawings of little cheerful fairy-beings I liked to draw.

One time I made the three-hour trip to see her at the nursing home. I was sitting on the side of her hospital bed and a nurse had propped her fragile little body next to mine. Because it hurt Bubby Ceile to sit up, she asked me to put her back down in the bed. As I started to help her, the nurse came by and told me it was really important for her to sit up, even for a few minutes, to help prevent bedsores. Then, I looked back at Bubby Ceile who was pleading with me to help her lie down.

I wanted to do the right thing, but I felt really torn. I didn't know what the right thing was. I decided the right thing was to honor Bubby Ceile's wishes. I couldn't stand to see her in such pain. So I put her back down in the bed.

Years have passed since that incident and I still think about it. I realize I would have felt guilt-ridden forever if I hadn't done what I did. I had helped Bubby Ceile out of her immediate pain, and I'm so glad I didn't listen to the nurse.

Some time later, at Bubby Ceile's funeral, I clearly heard her say to me as I looked at the simple pine coffin, "So, this is someone's idea of a bed?" It made me smile, in spite of all the tears.

Bubby Ceile now comes to me in my dreams where I can feel her presence strongly. These dreams usually happen when I am going through some difficult life passage. Recently, during a particularly rough time, she came to me with a bouquet of flowers.

I am grateful to still receive her love and support. She gives me hope and encouragement to continue on my life's journey. And every time I pick up a bottle of vitamins or hear a seam split, I think of her.

"All the good things you want for yourself should come true."
—Ceile Peyser

~~~ Steps to Happiness NOW! ~~~

105) Just because your family tree looks like shrubbery doesn't mean you should get out the hedge clippers

Nobody's perfect in a family. Some love us while others aren't capable of it. Some are opinionated. Others are eccentric. Some get along. Others don't. Regardless, each person makes an impact on our life. Appreciate each one for doing the best she can, in spite of all the cabbage she made you eat or because she dressed you funny when you were little.

106) Dig up a pile of good memories for a change

Out of all your childhood experiences, what are the memories of your family you truly cherish? Who brings a smile to your face when you think about him or her? Scan your memory banks for memories of your relatives doing or saying things that made you laugh. Remember the fun times.

107) Say "boo" to your fears

Fears are often passed down from generation to generation. Do you have any of the same fears as someone in your family? It's amazing how other people's fears can stick to us. Overcoming an inherited fear can be a lifelong process. If you are stuck in fear, trace its origins. Where did it start? Fears are meant to help keep us safe. The question is, does the fear still serve us, or is it just a tired old ghost?

108) Never let anything bug you

The more you let things bug you, the more bugs will show up in your life. The larger the problem, the bigger the bug. The way to repel bugs is to let go of the things bugging you. Easy. Piece of cake. OOPS, forget the cake—don't want bugs.

When Squirrels Take the Elevator and Fish Start to Sing

IT'S STORY TIME...

If St. Francis had been Jewish, he would have been my grandfather, Sam Fourman. My mother's father was very kind-hearted and had a deep love for animals. His bathtub often served as the rehabilitation ward for all kinds of winged and four-legged creatures in need of care. On his way home each night, he constantly fed stray dogs and cats with leftovers from the kitchens he worked in.

When my grandpa was old, he couldn't see very well. Still, everyday, he'd go outside and call the squirrels. At the sound of his kissy-call, all the squirrels would jump out of the trees and make a beeline, or rather, a squirrel-line, to him. The blue jays came too. The squirrels would take peanuts right out of his hands and the blue jays would jump on the bench next to him.

Once, a baby squirrel followed him inside his apartment building. My grandpa didn't see him. He took the elevator up to the second floor, walked down the long corridor to the last apartment, and rang the bell for my grandma Ida to open the door.

My grandma smiled when she saw the squirrel and told my grandpa, so back they went down the elevator.

It was because of animals that my parents met and fell in love. My mother was out walking her dog and my father was out looking for his, because it had just run away. They met on a street corner, started talking, and got married six months later. They've been together for forty-six years. So animals are a good thing.

I've always loved animals, too. One time, a little bird flew into a building where I was working. I helped get the bird out, but it kept flying back in. It was a finch, an exotic finch, not one I recognized as indigenous to the area.

I figured it had escaped from someone and probably wouldn't be able to survive much longer on its own. A coworker walked over to it and picked it up. We improvised a cage out of a raffle bin made out of wire netting. That night I brought it home.

I bought it a nice cage, a beautiful bird condo with birdie toys and special treats. The problem was, I can't stand to see anything in a cage. The bird couldn't stand it either.

So within two days, my apartment became one giant birdhouse. The front of the birdcage was open all the time, so he could fly in to eat, but was free to fly out whenever he wanted.

This little four-inch, no-pound bird changed my life forever. I named him Sweet Pea, because he was the sweetest little thing. He ate out of my hand and sang to me. Every night around 7:30 P.M., he'd fly up to a hoop in the living-room window, point his beak down and his little tushy up, and go to sleep. The angle at which he slept looked very severe. I'd say, "The bird's tipped for the night."

Sweet Pea loved to build nests all over the house. One time I had left a kitchen cabinet open, and when I returned home he was in the process of building a nest in the cheese grater. If I closed the cabinet, he'd dive-bomb it, trying to get in, so finally I just left it open.

Since I'm a weaver, and so was he, there was no lack of materials for nest building. He used fishing line, feathers, dead leaves, dried flowers and stems, cotton batting, yarn, lint, Q-tips, twist-ties, and dental floss. For a four-inch bird, he made eagle-sized nests that were truly a work of art.

I learned how to love unconditionally because of Sweet Pea. Once, I found him hanging upside down, his tiny leg caught in fine strands of thread. As I tried to hold him to get the threads undone, he freaked, clamped his little beak into the center of my palm, and wouldn't let go. It really hurt. I got a pair of scissors and made one cut in the main thread from which he was hanging, which allowed him to fly away to work the rest of the strands off himself.

After that traumatic experience (for both of us), he stopped eating out of my hand. I missed that little birdie closeness. I tried to send him psychic messages that I had been trying to help him and loved him and would never hurt him. Forget it. His psychic receptors were closed. He didn't trust me.

I decided I would keep on loving him, even if he never came to me again. As the weeks went by, this seemed more and more likely. It was difficult to let go of the need to have his love. But I did. I just let him be and continued to love him no matter what.

Then one day, over six months later, he flew near me. This was a big moment. Within days, he was eating out of my hand again as though nothing had ever happened. I don't know what shifted in his little birdie self to make him trust me again, but I'm glad he did.

I made up a little song I used to sing to him. You can tell by the quality of the lyrics that I have a unique ability for expressing sentiment. There were dance steps too, but I think I'll skip that part.

"I love my little birdie,
My birdie that I love.
I love my little birdie.
I'll always love my Sweet Pea."

Great poem, huh? At least the meaning is clear.

Sweet Pea went to birdie heaven in November of '92. I miss the sound of his tiny wings flapping as he'd fly through the living room. I miss the song he sang every morning when he woke up. I miss watching him splash water in every possible direction when he'd take his little birdie baths, and I even miss the teeny, tiny poops that decorated everything that wasn't covered.

Over the last two years, a pair of finches has been nesting in a fern on my front porch. I've always wondered if it could be Sweet Pea coming around again in a new birdie form. Whether it is Sweet Pea or not, it is comforting to me to know the birdies feel safe around me and my home.

Okay, now I hear you asking about my poem for Louis, King Hoo, and Toby—the fish. Since you asked so nicely...

> "Fishy, fishy, fishy.
> Fishy, fishy, fish.
> Fishy, fishy, fishy.
> Fishy, fishy, fish-fish-fish.
> Fishy, fishy, fish-fish-fish."

You can cha-cha to the last two lines. One. Two. Cha-cha-cha. One. Two. Fish-fish-fish.

Toby really likes the words. He always sings along. For King Hoo it's an emotional experience. Sometimes we sing it in rounds. Louis starts.

At this point, however, I want something I can pet. The fish won't cooperate. Singing is one thing; being petted is quite another.

So, I've been asking Santa to bring me a winky dog, but it hasn't appeared yet. Realization—I'm Jewish. Okay, now who am I supposed to ask? The Easter Bunny's out of the question, and I'm too old for the tooth fairy.

Come on, Santa, give me a break. I want a little winky dog.

What's a winky dog? A little "winky" thing. Not a big dog, just a little winky dog, something about the size of a miniature wiener dog. Does that explain it?

One day, I described my ideal winky dog to my landlady. It definitely couldn't be yippy-yappy. It had to be a loving, little healer dog who enjoyed kids, adults, and other animals. It would also be nice if it didn't shed, have doggy breath, or come with fleas. As my landlady listened to my description of my dream doggy, she said, "You don't want just any old dog. You want a dog soulmate."

She was right. I wanted a dog soulmate. And I wanted my winky dog to find me. My bird found me and I wanted my winky dog to find me, too.

So I'm in no hurry. As with any relationship, I know that finding the right soulmate takes time. Meanwhile I'll take myself over to the park for walks until my winky dog finds its winky way to me.

Animals never make fun of your poetry.

~~~ Steps to Happiness NOW! ~~~

109) Maybe some tails are better left untold

One time at work, I had an acute attack of deadpan seriousness. So for relief, I found an old piece of fur and stuck it out the back of my pants like a tail. Instantly, I felt happier. Then I got busy and forgot about it. Later on I went to the bathroom, and standing to flush, saw a dead rat in the toilet. Actually, it was the tail. Even though I rescued it, I haven't worn it since. Animals are lucky. Their tails don't fall off.

110) Unless the dog launched a stink bomb, spend time in the company of animals

Every animal is our mirror. Some remind us of our own precious innocence or spark the love in our hearts. Others bring out our sense of compassion, or our sense of fear or respect. Think of an animal you like. What do you like about it? Chances are that's what you like about yourself, too. Are you a friendly animal or do you bite?

111) Find freedom in your life

Animals can make a world of difference. One time during a meltdown, I met a very special horse. "Freedom" would stand totally still, allowing me to pet his nose or rest my face against his while I cried. Every time I visited Freedom, the grief absolutely vanished. Now that I'm happier, all he cares about are carrots. However, when I really needed help, Freedom was there.

112) Aspire to be the kind of person your dog thinks you are

If you have a pet, how do you think your pet views you? Are you the greatest thing this side of a porterhouse steak? Or are you merely the walking can-opener? Either way, I bet your pet thinks you're the best. Isn't it nice to know you're appreciated? Ask your family members or your boss to appreciate you just like your pet does, except don't settle for a dead mouse dropped at your feet.

How to Impress a Potential Landlord

It's Story Time...

While waiting for my winky dog to miraculously appear, I decided I might as well take the landlords' twelve-year-old, deaf springer spaniel, Cookie, with me when I went out for my daily walks in the park.

Cookie, who had been stuck in that yard for years, delighted in our adventures around the duck pond. I became her passage to fun and freedom and she became my surrogate doggy companion. With the passage of time, it was pretty clear—I was "her person," and she was "my dog." I had found my soulmate.

There was only one problem. She wasn't my dog. She was *their* dog! Although, I tried my darndest not to get too attached, I couldn't help myself. Cookie was flea-ridden and dirty. Pinecones dangled from the matted fur on her long, floppy ears. Bits of twigs were embedded in the fur on her legs. She had flaky skin and God knows what else. It didn't matter. I loved her.

One day, the landlords dumped a rather big surprise on me. They had decided to give my cottage to their daughter. Oh my God! I'd been there for over five years. All of a sudden I was getting the bootsky. What about Cookie? I couldn't bear the thought of being without her.

Timidly, I asked the landlords if they would let me take her with me. Without a second of hesitation they said, "Yes."

In that moment, a new sense of joy was born in my heart. Instantly, I became a dog mommy. I brought Cookie to the vet, put goop in her infected ears, put other goop in her infected eyes, gave her nine thousand baths, and fed her essential fatty oils, grape-seed extract, acidophilus, and all these other things which made her coat nice and sleek. Pretty soon, this raga-muffin old dog was transformed into a born-again puppy. Nothing made me happier than to see her smile.

Finding a new place to rent with a dog, however, was turning out to be no easy task. One day, a friend offered a suggestion: "Why not put together a "Renter's Resume" to give to prospective landlords?"

Great idea. Being a writer, I quickly whipped up a resume, not only highlighting my wonderful credentials as a tenant, but also including a section for Cookie's credentials. For example, she befriended cats. She was gentle with children. She got along well with other dogs. I went on and on about all of her wonderful qualities. Surely this resume would make a fantastic impression on any potential landlord. At the very least, it would make me stand out amidst all the other applicants vying for a place.

With this great resume in hand, Cookie and I went to check out our first possibility. When we arrived, we were greeted at the door by a big, long-haired, four-legged mixed breed. The two dogs quickly romped off to play.

Meanwhile, I stopped paying attention to the dogs and started moseying around the apartment, checking out the size of each room. The tiny place really didn't hold much appeal for me.

As I walked from room to room, all of a sudden I spotted something nasty in the middle of the kitchen floor. It was then that I noticed I had accidentally stepped in another pile of the stuff and had unknowingly smeared it deeply into the kitchen linoleum with my size 10 sneakers—obviously Cookie had cast her vote about the place, too.

After my profuse apologies, and time spent scraping my shoes and the linoleum clean, I left—the bag of evidence in one hand, the dog on a leash in the other. Cookie looked at the bag innocently as if to say, "What have you got there?" I didn't bother to hand the woman our great resume on the way out.

From then on I decided it would be best if Cookie stayed at home while I looked at places. It didn't seem to make any difference. I still couldn't find a place for the two of us and time was running out.

The weekend before I needed to move, I was invited to a picnic. Since I knew it would be attended by many people, I decided to perform yet another random act of chutzpah. So I taped a sign across my t-shirt which read: "Rental Home Needed August 1st. Inquire Within."

During the course of the picnic, a woman whom I had never met before walked up to me, smiling at the classified ad blaring across my chest. She had a room for rent in a beautiful house surrounded by nature. She also loved animals. In an instant, Cookie and I found our wonderful new home.

Always put your best foot forward, but be careful where you step.

~~~ Steps to Happiness NOW! ~~~

113) We are all here to be each other's angels

Miracles not only come through the hands of God, they also come through the hands of people. If you want something, tell the world. Let others know exactly what it is you want. Someone may have the perfect resource or contact you need. If you don't tell others what you need or want, you are potentially denying them the opportunity to be an angel in your life.

114) Value the unexpected twists and turns of life

Transitions can bring us to a much more wonderful place in our lives than we could have ever imagined. Yet most of us aren't eager to change anything that disrupts our current sense of security. That's why we need a catalyst, a person or a situation that serves to willingly or unwillingly move us in our new direction. Sometimes we may dislike or even hate what catalyzes us; however, a catalyst is often a blessing in disguise.

115) Honey, where's the cheese?

This is an inside joke in my family. One time, my father opened the door of the fridge, and staring inside, called out to my mother, "Honey, where's the cheese?" I happened to be standing near him at the time and saw the cheese sitting right there, front and center. What we want could be right in front of our eyes, although we may not see it.

116) Love something

It doesn't matter if the object of your loving kindness is a human being, a plant, or an animal. That which is nurtured grows. If it is nurtured, it will flourish. Love is the greatest miracle. It is one gift we can give to anyone or anything just by our smile or a kind word.

The Dog Bed That Dropped from Heaven

It's Story Time...

Once we moved into our new home, Cookie quickly chose the space under my computer desk as her den. This seemed like the perfect cozy spot—protected overhead by the top of the desk with Randy's toes tucked under her nice warm body as she typed.

The only problem was Cookie's bed. The old green floor pillow was a little too small. So she slept at odd angles with her head and part of her body pressed against the floor.

Cookie's thirteenth birthday was just a week away. She deserved a good-sized bed, however I couldn't afford one. Then a few days later, a miracle happened.

Cookie and I were heading over to a grocery store. Since every single space in the parking lot was taken, we had to circle around a number of times before a space finally opened up.

As Cookie and I got out of the car, I saw a lady approach two men standing beside a truck. Although I couldn't hear what she asked them, I could see them shaking their heads "no." Assuming she needed directions, I offered my help.

It turned out the woman wasn't lost. What she had asked the men was if either of them had a dog. It turned out she sold dog beds and just happened to have one in the back of her car. What a gimmick—selling dog beds out of the back of a car. She immediately launched into her sales pitch. It was brand-new and filled with sweet-smelling cedar and chopped foam. The flannel cover could be unzipped for easy washing. It had been returned to a store and was in perfect condition. For some reason, it couldn't be resold once it had been returned.

A little warily, I asked, "How much?"

And she replied, "Oh, no, I just want to give it away!"

So Cookie got her brand-new dog bed, and I cried with gratitude the entire way home. There was no doubt in my mind God had felt the sincerity of my wish and provided for my doggy girl in this unique and almost unbelievable way.

That night, Cookie plopped herself down on her new bed, assuming the position of a queen dog on her throne. I was filled with happiness, thinking about how she could finally stretch out in total comfort on a nice big bed. The next morning when I woke up, however, the truth was, Cookie had positioned herself in such a way that part of her body still dangled over the edge at an odd angle and her head was pressed against the floor.

I guess it's true what they say—"You can't teach an old dog new tricks."

God hears your tiniest wishes.

~~~ Steps to Happiness NOW! ~~~

117) Sometimes the most direct route is the circuitous route

Life often doesn't seem to work like this: "I want X, therefore, I get X." Life seems to work more like this: "I want X, but I got Y, which led me to Q, which led me to Z, and then, voila, X showed up on my doorstep!" You never know who or what will lead you to a vital connection to help you get what you truly desire. Stay open when unusual or unforeseen opportunities come your way.

118) Miracles respond to patience and divine right timing

If you are grasping for a miracle, it's bound not to happen. You can't manipulate God into giving anything to you. Your sense of right timing and God's sense of right timing might be completely different. Have patience. Be grateful for every moment. Know that everything unfolds in its own right time, including your life.

119) Give voice to your tiniest of wishes

For some reason, it seems as though our softest, littlest wishes are the ones most likely to be fulfilled the quickest. These are the kinds of wishes that sometimes glide across our mind and then disappear. There's some sort of magic involved in wishing for something, then letting it go without being attached to an outcome.

120) Notice and appreciate moments of synchronicity

Synchronicity is that wonderful place where magic and grace intersect. Moments of synchronicity serve to remind us that we are not alone, and that there is a God who does, indeed, intervene on our behalf. Think about the synchronicities you've experienced in your life and give thanks for them.

SECTION 4

WHO'S OUT THERE?

A Peek at the Cosmos

- ❋ In this section, we're going to increase our altitude and head for the Heavens.

- ❋ It is our personal connection with the Divine that enriches our earthly experience and often provides the answers we're seeking.

- ❋ Many of us believe in some sort of greater presence that guides or influences our lives. Through prayer, meditation, self-inquiry (or sometimes begging), we'll search for answers or support from "Up There."

- ❋ In this section we'll also discover how Murphy (of Murphy's Law) is in cahoots with God! Stay tuned.

God Is a Potato

It's Story Time...

When I was four-years-old, I believed that God was a potato. Here's how I reached this profound, enlightening conclusion. One day, I was helping my mother peel potatoes. She was showing me the buds that sometimes grow out of potatoes and she told me these were called "eyes."

Later that day, the subject of God came up. I remember my mother explaining to me that God was this great being in heaven who watched over us all the time. No matter where we were in the world, God could always see us.

Aha! In the same day, I had learned that potatoes have eyes and that God can see us all the time.

"Hmmm. If potatoes have eyes, and God has eyes, this must mean that God is a potato." It made perfect sense!

I even worked out what God looked like. I remembered the image of yet another eye, the one in the pyramid on the dollar bill. So I visualized a potato, standing vertically, with the eye in the pyramid on the potato's face. This is what God looked like. The Cyclopsian eye could move in any direction so it could always see me, although the potato appeared to be stationary.

The potato-God stayed with me for many years. I didn't think of it as a particularly loving or protecting entity, just as something that could always see me, so I'd better be careful and only do good things.

Answers to questions you're thinking of at this point—

No, I never went to McDonalds to pray, and yes, of course Mr. Potatohead was an abomination of the likeness of the Lord.

~The Keeper of the World's Balloons~

My friend, Oshara, remembers the first time she was given a balloon as a toddler. It was big! It was red! It was wonderful! And it was filled with helium.

Of course, like any two-year-old, she was devastated when she let go of the string and the balloon rose into the sky and wouldn't come back.

Oshara's mom came to the rescue. She told Oshara the balloon was going up to heaven where it would be with God. Oshara immediately filled with hope as she asked her mother, "When I die, can I get my balloon back?"

So this is what Oshara's world cosmology looked like: "I pictured God as the keeper of all the world's balloons. When we died, we'd get all our balloons back. That was God's main function; keeping our balloons for us until that time came and then surprising us with them all."

POTATO? BALLOON KEEPER?
BALLOON KEEPER? POTATO?

The debate over God goes on.

Ashes to Ashes and Dust to Dust—
If You Have to Dispose of It,
Do What You Must

My brother has a 125-gallon fish tank. Whenever one of his fish dies, he takes it outside and throws it over the fence into the alleyway for some meandering feline to feast upon.

One day, my four-year-old niece was watching a TV show in which a character died. This prompted her to ask my brother about death. My brother told her about death and funerals and burials.

My niece pondered his words, then asked, "Why don't we just throw them over the fence?"

Make a date with God and do some talking. Remember to listen.

~~~~ Steps to Happiness NOW! ~~~~

121) If you need help, open your arms and ask

There's an old quote, "If you don't feel close to God anymore, who moved?" When life is hard, we often wonder why God bailed out on us. One time, in utter exasperation, I asked my friend Oshara, "When is God going to help me, already?" And she replied, "You've answered your own question—'already'."

122) Have a talk with God—remember to listen

God and I have been getting together for chats on a nearby mountainside. For an hour or two, I talk, pray, demand, sob, negotiate, scream, and surrender. Patiently, God listens. When it's all out of me, I get quiet so I can listen. Sometimes I sit for a long time, just breathing and absorbing the beauty of my surroundings in silence. Then I give thanks and leave, feeling renewed and at peace.

123) Be careful about what you ask for—you just might get it

One night, I dreamt that the word, "INSIST," was spelled out on a Scrabble board. I woke up thinking, "What do I want so much in my life that I'd be willing to insist upon it?" To insist meant that I'd be so clear, there'd be no room for doubt or hesitation. When I insist upon something now, I always say, "God, I ask for this or better," just in case God has a better plan in mind.

124) God is watching out for you—did you forget?

One time I screamed at God, "I've done all this intense inner work for months and I need to be rewarded!" (I was insisting.) Upon leaving the mountain, I was instantly rewarded. I met Freedom the horse's owner at the base of the trail, and she offered to teach me how to take him out by myself. After the incredibly synchronistic meeting with her, I meekly said, "Thank you, God. I guess you were listening after all."

It Wasn't a Dream. I Swear. I Was Asleep. But It Wasn't a Dream.

It's Story Time...

I was taken to Heaven—not someone's idea of Heaven: this was the real thing, the Yankee Stadium of the Holiest of Holies, the Club Med of Spirit.

Prior to this I'd never really thought about or given much credence to this place called Heaven. To me, Heaven was no more real than Santa Claus, Bambi, or the Tooth Fairy.

This is what happened: I snuggled into my waterbed and fell into a deep sleep. The next thing I knew I was in a taxi. The driver asked me where I wanted to go.

"Highway 1, south to Pacifica."

Did the taxi driver listen? No. Instead he headed up into the sky.

"Whoa," I thought, "this taxi driver knows some pretty fancy shortcuts to Pacifica."

Then the taxi disappeared and the driver and I were just standing in the air—not hovering or flying—just standing there as though air was a perfectly solid substance to stand upon.

I was witnessing something totally magnificent, glorious, stunning. "Get the video camera quick!"

The clouds looked prettier than any clouds I'd ever flown through in a plane. Looking at them closer, I could distinguish the shapes of angels. The fresh crisp blues of the sky, the sparkling whites of the clouds, and the soft glow of light from the angels were brighter than any colors I had ever seen.

The air had a crisp crystalline quality to it with no evidence of L.A. smog. There was no sound or movement. Everything felt glowingly alive. I could see hundreds of angels, each at the center of their own individual cloud condos. In the distance a great white light poured into one cloud in particular.

Although there seemed to be no movement of any kind, I sensed there was much going on. It appeared that no one there ever took a lunch break.

Heaven was utterly still and pristinely quiet. In fact, the quiet in Heaven was so pure, it is hard to put into words.

Now I understand why we need to become silent to hear God. It is so quiet in Heaven. The yapping inside our heads during our everyday lives keeps out the subtle, beautiful messages the angels want most to give us.

I then imagined what it must be like to be an angel:

Here I am in this pure state, traveling down to Earth on a light beam moving faster than the elevator at Macy's. As I get closer and closer to the Earth, I notice that the energy around the planet isn't as quiet and sparkly and pristine as where I come from. It feels dense, as though an invisible barrier has been set in place to slow me down. The thoughts manufactured by human beings as they fret and worry about their lives and the noise made by the machines they have manufactured seem to have created this force field. It is not easy for me to get through it.

I want to give you a message, touch your heart, bring you comfort. However, by the time I get here, I'm competing with leaf blowers, grumbling trucks with back-up beepers, football games on TV, and children who won't eat their peas. You're busy, stressed, and preoccupied. What's an angel to do?

Wait, I guess. That angel's got to wait for our minds to quiet down enough so we can hear what they want to tell us. The quieter we get, the better chance they have of getting through.

The dream experience continued. It was time for me to leave Heaven. I listened to myself say, "Okay, it's time to go back to my body," and then I felt myself coming back. I was completely aware of the process as I clicked back into my body. Still asleep, I acknowledged I was back in my body and said to myself, "All right, I'm going to wake up now." Then I opened my eyes and was wide awake.

I had gone from a sleeping state to a waking state while maintaining consciousness the whole time. It was so simple. This experience made me feel that the transition from birth to death or from death to birth is just as simple.

Now I believe that changing from one state of reality to another state of reality (like changing from a dream state to a waking state, or from being alive to being dead) is just as easy as being able to say, "Now I'm here, and now I'm here—somewhere else, but still here in a different here." Pretty soon you're here, there, and everywhere, and the Beatles are writing a song about you. Wherever we are, we are conscious and fine the whole time. Of this, I am sure.

So do I leave a tip for the taxi driver? If so, how much?

Begin with a breath and a prayer.

~~~ Steps to Happiness NOW! ~~~

125) Turn inward to touch the divine

There's a quote that says, "Prayer is us talking to God, and meditation is God answering." You can hear the voice of Spirit when you get quiet inside. One way to fine-tune your hearing is to sit in silence. Light a candle and listen to the sound of a silent flame. Just sit with the silence. Breathe and listen. Divine inspiration may come in a whisper, so be open, ready, and willing.

126) Ask to be guided

Isn't it interesting that in spite of significant differences, most religions around the world believe in angels? We all have friends in spirit form. Call on your angels and guides often. Invite them to take a walk with you in nature. Allow them to enter your consciousness. Ask for more contact and be open to whatever you receive. Keep asking. What you ask for will grow.

127) Go to sleep, count some sheep

One of the easiest ways to be in touch with our spirit guides is through the dream state. As you go to sleep each night, ask to meet your Higher Guide in dreamland. Then start counting sheep until you fall asleep or the sheep go home. Do this every night. A guide might appear as a person or even as an animal. In my case, my guides often give me visual messages in the form of puns. For example, dreams about Nazis mean, what am I "not see"-ing?

128) "Are you a good witch or a bad witch?"

Just because they're not wearing a body doesn't mean they know more than we do. It's a multipurpose Universe out there with its share of disembodied, astral creeps as well as its angelic beings. Learn to discern. I once asked Oshara, who talks to her spirit pals regularly, "How can you tell if they're good or bad?" Her response was, "When they're good, you always feel loved. If the love's not there, say 'bye-bye'."

The Message on The Mountain

It's Story Time...

Over the years I'd heard about a mountain in Northern California, called Mt. Shasta, which drew spiritual seekers from around the world. Since I had always wondered about the mountain, when I was invited to join a group of people who were driving up to Shasta to do a prayer walk, I jumped at the opportunity. Who knew what mystical experience might be awaiting me there? At the very least it sounded like a nice way to spend a weekend, tuning inward, being in nature, and surrounded by a group of people in thoughtful contemplation.

This was also going to be one of my first experiences of camping. *Camping*. What better way to feel closer to nature than by sleeping under the open stars? It sounded good—in theory.

After a long drive, a friend and I arrived in Shasta at 1:00 in the morning, so we decided we'd better spend our first night camping at the Best Western. Flush toilets, showers, a king-sized bed, HBO. I liked camping.

The next morning we drove fourteen miles up the mountain, and finding a little nook and cranny to call our own, set up our tiny two-person tent. As I carried the compact cooler filled with hummus and pita bread to our campsite, I felt like a rugged mountain woman. Camping was so cool.

We located the rest of our group, who were in the midst of a potluck. It was important we knew the rules.

"Make sure you lock all your food in your car at night because of the bears," one said.

"Bears?" My eyebrows nearly reached my hairline.

"Also, no peeing or pooping in the woods. Go up to the outhouse if you have to go, okay?"

"Outhouse? What? No flush toilet? No shower? Wait a minute. I'm rough. I'm tough. I can carry the pita bread and hummus back to the car every night. A rugged mountain woman can handle this for a few days. Bears? Hmmm."

We joined the happy campers around the barbecue. I especially liked the fried potatoes and helped myself to a heaping portion of seconds. Then we spent the rest of the day frolicking near our campsite, watching the millions of chipmunks at play, pointing at pretty flowers, and having a Kumbaya kind of experience.

That night, while lying down on my twelve-inch-thick mattress pad (no half-inch egg-carton foam, wimpy camping mattress pad for me!), I started getting cramps. My guess was it was something I'd eaten.

That night, it seemed as though all the stars in the Universe were visible at once. And I got to see them over and over again as I made countless stumbling trips, doubled over in the dark, up to the outhouse. Camping? Hmmm.

The next morning, I was quickly able to identify the culprit. It was the potatoes. These potatoes were not God! They were evil potatoes, cooked in butter—the Satan of the lactose-intolerant.

Everyone was preparing for the hike up the mountain. Water bottles were being filled and sunscreen applied. We were given the game plan. First, we would hike about two and a half hours up the mountain to a plateau. At that point there would be a trail of large flat rocks. This is where our prayer walk would begin. From this point, we would proceed in silence at our own pace, in whatever form of prayer or contemplation we liked.

Two and a half hours, huh? I didn't know if I could go two and a half minutes without an outhouse. Then I remembered I was a rugged mountain woman, and no crampy diarrhea was going to keep me down.

We drove to the starting point, a trail called "Bunny Flat." I liked the Bunny part. That sounded pleasant enough. However, I couldn't imagine why a trail straight up a mountain was named, "Flat." We started up the trail, and within minutes, people were off at their own pace. I had to rest many times, but was pleasantly surprised I didn't have to make any emergency pit stops behind the scraggly pines.

Finally, I reached the plateau point and was delighted to see a lodge complete with picnic tables, a clean outhouse, a large patio, and a hose, spouting fresh, running water coming straight from the peak. Our group converged to eat lunch and rest on the bright green grass. Feeling revitalized, we prepared for the next part of our journey.

The large flat stones loomed forward in a singular, curvy sweep heading further up the mountain over peaks and out of sight. Walking on the stones, the terrain changed. The land was sparsely dotted with small outcroppings of rock, the ground looked dry, and there were no more trees. The air felt alive and fresh in my lungs even though the landscape grew more and more desolate.

As I stood on the first stone, I grew very silent and closed my eyes. My arms hanging loosely by my side, the palms of my hands facing outward, I listened.

Within a few minutes I heard an affirmation quietly pop into my head, and upon taking a slow, intentional breath, I whispered it into the air. "I release the need to receive attention through pain."

As I spoke these words I found I was softly crying. I took the next step, repeating the affirmation. "I release the need to receive attention through pain." Another deep breath, followed by more tears.

I continued in silence, first noticing, then losing track of the others as each of us moved in rhythm with our own inner worlds. Another affirmation took hold. "I am grateful. I give thanks for all that is. I give thanks for everything." I looked around and gave thanks to the stones, to the mountain, and to the life all around me.

A large boulder hugging the stone trail beckoned me to come sit for awhile. Assuming a comfortable position on the rock, I sipped some water while peacefully admiring the view. After a nice rest, I felt ready to continue onward.

As I slid off of the boulder, I was suddenly in excruciating pain. As I let out a scream, a bee flew out of my shoe. It had stung me on the bottom of my foot!

How do these things happen? Here I was over two and a half hours up a mountain after having just released the need to receive attention through pain and I had just been stung on the bottom of my foot. What are the odds?

I couldn't walk. I was sure I'd have to be carried down the mountain on a litter by a team of park rangers or maybe they'd need a helicopter to transport me off the mountain. So much for releasing the need for attention.

A few women from my group rushed over to assist. One held her hands about six inches away from my foot and did Reiki, an ancient healing technique of applying energy to a wound. The other started toning, making sounds which went up the scale from the lowest low to the highest high. At the same time, she made a spiral gesture with her hand over the sting, as if energetically, she was pulling the pain out.

As she repeated this gesture, I suddenly felt a sharp ping, which made me jump a little bit. Then the pain completely subsided. Either I had been healed by their toning and energy work, or the stinger had popped out. I didn't know which. All I knew was the pain was gone and no one had ever physically touched my foot.

Since I was no longer in pain, they left. As soon as they were out of sight, fear filled my mind. Suppose my foot swelled? Would the pain start up again? Could I get all the way back down the mountain on my own? Would I be stranded?

Fortunately, one of the older members of our group was ready to head back and offered to accompany me on the way down. I felt relieved. At least I was not alone. We walked slowly, sometimes in tandem and sometimes in solitude, giving space to our own thoughts. By the time we got back to the parking lot I felt tired, but completely fine.

Eventually my driving buddy returned and we decided to drive into town to stock up on more hummus. As we approached the grocery store, I spotted a red Swiss army knife lying on the sidewalk. Someone had carved the letter "B" (as in bee?) right in front of the red cross insignia. Clearly a message: "Bee Positive!" What a great gift.

The next afternoon, as my friend and I prepared to leave, we attempted to start up the car. Nothing happened. The engine finally kicked over. Relief. Then shifting into reverse, the gears gave a groan and all of a sudden the shift thing (hey, I'm not mechanically inclined, okay?) froze up completely. No forward. No reverse. No nothing. It was Sunday, which also meant no working mechanics. And it was the little town of Shasta, which further meant no taxis, no buses, and no rental car agencies. Fortunately, AAA said they'd come right over—in about two hours.

Eventually the AAA truck arrived, and the driver hooked up his hookey-things to the back end of the car. As he attempted to drag the car backward, something unlocked, and suddenly we had the use of the gears—at least all of the ones that moved forward. We weren't sure about reverse.

We practically flew out of Shasta, making sure never to go in reverse, and made it back to my home five hours later on one tank of gas.

After dropping me off at my door, my friend drove another forty-five minutes further to her home. Then something strange happened. The car wouldn't stop. Even when she turned it off, it kept lunging forward. Eventually, she put on the emergency brake, got out of the car, and disconnected the battery. Finally, the car surrendered.

So that was the Shasta experience. In spite of the outhouses, evil potatoes, lack of showers, threat of bears, challenging lessons from a bee, getting cold in the middle of the night, and the broken-down car, I returned home feeling refreshed and exhilarated. After all, how could there ever be anything a rugged mountain woman like myself couldn't possibly handle after an adventure like that?

Sometimes there is no going back and you can only go forward—even when it doesn't seem like you can move at all.

~~~ Steps to Happiness NOW! ~~~

129) Imagine yourself living in the present

Fear is rarely about the present moment. It's usually about the anticipation of something not happening right now, and that may or may not happen in the future. So be in this moment. Look at your surroundings. Feel this moment. Smell this moment. Touch this moment. You are not in any other moment. Where are you? You are here. Now.

130) Make time for the sacred unfolding of who you are

Listen to the calling of the Sacred within you. Find that quiet place where you can touch the Source, that place which feeds the deepest longing of your soul. Visit this place often. It will always nurture you, and whenever you wish to return to it, it will always be there. Invite your angels and guides to join you too. They never return an RSVP signed, "Sorry, I can't attend."

131) Wherever you go, you are standing on holy ground

One of the best places to hear the calling of the Sacred is in nature, so do earthy kinds of things. Go hug a tree (you can tell people it's your latent hippie-granola-self emerging) or sit by a riverbed. Listen to the birds sing, or touch a soft petal to your cheek. Fill your lungs with fresh air and breathe with reverence. Walk softly on the earth—let the tiny flowers live.

132) Send your prayers up to heaven on the branches of a tree

Pretend your feet are the roots of a tree, heading deep below the earth. Your body is the trunk, sturdy and strong, and your arms are leafy branches heading toward the sky. Let your prayers be carried up to heaven on the tips of your leafy branches. You can hug a real tree and send your prayers up that way too. Do whichever is easier. If something nests in your hair, you are doing it right.

The Indisputable Proof That Someone up There Has a Sense of Humor

IT'S STORY TIME...

I'd swear my friend Carol has a pipeline to the angelic forces. One night while talking on the phone, Carol said, "Not only are there many angels working with you, they're looking out for you, even to the point where they are concerned about the littlest details which affect your life."

Carol went on to tell me that these angels loved me so much that they even cared about how the light shone through my window in the morning. They cared about the smell in the air as I walked out the door. They cared about the tree branch extending its leafy arm to greet me as I walked in the yard. They cared about the sounds reaching my ears.

As Carol told me this, I started to feel special. I felt loved by all of creation.

Even though it was almost two in the morning, Carol suggested that before I drifted off to sleep, I go outside and hug a tree.

So I snuck outside like someone on a clandestine mission. A giant redwood beckoned to me. I wrapped my arms around its trunk and settled into a long embrace. Eventually I turned around and leaned my back against the trunk, continuing to absorb all that good tree energy.

Carol had also told me to surround myself with some pleasant aromas. There was a giant rosemary bush in the yard. As I went to pick a sprig or two, I imagined those beautiful loving angels walking with me. I thought about how they were guiding my every move. I felt so loved, so cared about, so special, so protected. All of a sudden I realized something: I had just stepped in doggy-doo.

"Okay, I want to know which angel was on duty that moment?! Was this the one angel in charge of all the dog-doo in the world? Did this angel handle cow pies as well? Or maybe it was a dud angel who should be reported to a supervisor.

So many questions. I want answers! I know. I'll consult the receptionist at the Pearly Gate."

"Knock, knock."

"Who's there?"

"Randy."

"Randy who?"

"Randy from the Earth plane."

"Randy from the Earth plane who?"

"Randy from the Earth plane who wants to know who handles the doggy-doo on my planet?"

"Probably the pooper-scooper-uppers."

"No, that's not what I mean. I want to know if there's an angel whose function is to help connect the foot of a human being with a pile of doggy-doo."

"Let's see. Why don't you try the DEPARTMENT FOR ANSWERS TO LIFE'S BIGGEST QUESTIONS. It's the second cloud down on the right."

"Thanks."

"Knock knock."

"Who's there?"

"Randy."

"Randy who?"

"Randy who wants some big answers."

"Good. You've come to the right place. Come in."

"Thanks."

"What's your question?"

"I want to know if there's an angel whose sole function is to connect the foot of a human being with a pile of doggy-doo."

"Hmmm, I don't have that information offhand. It's not a question I can remember having heard before. I'll have to consult the catalog.

"Let's see what we've got under the D's. Dancers, Devas, Dish-doers, Dinner assisters, Divers, Drivers, Do-gooders, Door openers, Drama queens. Sorry, there's no listing under doggy-doo. Why don't you try the ETERNAL MYSTERIES DEPARTMENT? Perhaps they can help you. They're the next flight up, and three clouds down on the left."

"Thanks."

"Knock knock."

"Who's there?"

"Randy."

"Randy who?"

"Randy who has a question no one seems to know the answer to."

"Good. You've come to the right place. Come in."

"Thanks."

"What's your question?"

"I want to know if there's an angel whose sole function is to connect the foot of a human being with a pile of doggy-doo."

"Darned if I know. Let me ask some others in the department. Hey, Bermuda Triangle Group, do you know the answer?"

"Darned if we know."

"What about you, Pyramid Builder Investigators?"

"Darned if we know."

"Maybe the Return of the Messiah Committee. Do you guys know the answer?"

"Nope, darned if we know."

"Nobody seems to know the answers to anything up here!"

"That's why we're the ETERNAL MYSTERIES DEPARTMENT. I've got an idea. Why don't you try the DEPARTMENT OF SILLY MANEUVERS? You can just slide down that rainbow over there and you'll arrive at their front door."

"Wow, thanks."

"Knock knock."

"Who's there?"

"Randy."

"Randy who?"

"Randy who has a question no one seems to know the answer to."

"That sounds serious. I don't think we can help you."

"OOPS. Let me rephrase the question. Is there an angel in charge of doggy-doo?"

"That's better. You've come to the right place. Please come in."

"Thanks."

"In this department, seriousness is a no-no. We use humor to get our message across, and doggy-doo, being what it is, is a perfect medium for us to teach with. Do you know how many ways we can use doggy-doo to make a point?"

"God, I don't have a clue."

"Well, think about what happened to you. You actually learned a number of lessons from your experience. Can you tell me what you learned?"

"Let's see. I learned that it is okay for me to feel I'm special, as long as I remember that everyone else is special too. If I think it's just about me and me alone, I'll probably find myself in another pile of poop."

"That was a good one. What else?"

"I learned that I should watch where I step."

"Yes. Use your powers of discernment and keen observation. You'll know when something feels right and when it doesn't. What else did you learn?"

"I learned that I am the prime creator in my life. I'm the one who calls the shots and makes the decisions about what I want to create for me."

"That's true. When we're invited, we assist where we can. But you've got center stage. You're the director and it's your show."

"I also learned that just because I feel guided doesn't mean I can sit around and do nothing."

"There are times when you need to take action and there are times when you need to be still and let things unfold. Both are necessary and both are true."

"Wow. I guess I learned a lot from this experience."

"There's one more thing. You love to laugh. We want to make sure you don't take this all too seriously. Of course, the fuddy-duddies over at the DEPARTMENT OF HEAVY BROODING CONCERNS wouldn't agree with our philosophy. That's okay. There's something for everybody up here.

"Meanwhile, delight in the twinkle of the Universe. Life is more fun when you turn on your twinkler; so twinkle!"

"This has been an extremely rewarding conversation. Thanks for the insights."

"You're quite welcome. We want you to enjoy yourself. And when you forget, just remember, a little doggy-doo will doo ya."

"God, that's so silly."

"Silliness happens. That's what we're here for."

Express your silly self.

~~~ Steps to Happiness NOW! ~~~

133) Murphy's in cahoots with God

Why is it that the person who's afraid of fish bones (me) winds up with the only piece of fish with tiny bones in it? And why is it that the one who can't swim (again, me) gets caught in a whirlpool and has to be pulled out by a pregnant lifeguard? Situations that produce our greatest fears arise so we can free ourselves, because wherever we hold fear, energy doesn't flow. Thanks loads, Murphy.

134) Embrace the unexpected

Where we wind up might be very different from where we thought we were headed. There's a flow to the Universe, and there's a flow to our lives. We are not solely in control here. The only thing we're really in control of is not being in control. And yet, we're responsible for it all. Go figure.

135) Life is special—just ask someone who doesn't have one

I met a woman with a unique perspective. As a paralegal for a probate attorney, Martha Colburn realized that all of her clients were just as dead when she left work at night as they would be the next morning, so she decided never to bring the worries of her workday home with her. In the greater scheme of things, is anything really worth worrying about anyway?

136) Look forward to a new adventure that begins with today

Forget everything you know. This is a new moment! Who knows what this day will bring? It could bring more of the same old, same old, or it might just bring something terrific. Here's an experiment you can try, courtesy of my friend, Mahima. Say, "Wonderful things are happening to me today," frequently, with gusto, and notice what pops up in your life.

SECTION 5

CREATE A WORLD OF LOVE

Practice Intentional Acts of Kindness

- ❋ Our final section focuses on creating greater meaning in our lives by offering the gift of ourselves to a higher purpose.
- ❋ The smallest act of kindness can make a world of difference.
- ❋ Many people think that a closed heart is a safe heart. Actually, the opposite is true. It is only by sharing our hearts that we find true happiness.
- ❋ The act of giving opens the heart and fills it with love. And a heart overflowing with love is the safest in the Universe. It is also a heart that will know much happiness.

The Gift

IT'S STORY TIME...

Some years ago I came down with two viral conditions that half the country is suffering from and the other half says don't exist. I chewed eighty supplements a day to combat the Epstein-Barr and Cytomegola boogie monsters that devastated my body. This was a real feat for someone who's phobic about swallowing pills.

For two and a half years, I endured hearing things like, "What you need is exercise, there's nothing wrong with you."

For some reason I thought that having lost the ability to walk on my own would interfere with my ability to exercise, and I didn't need to work up a sweat because I already had one from a constant low-grade fever.

My only trip out of bed each day was to get my noontime home-delivered meal. This is when I learned that the real purpose of walls was to have something to lean against so I could reach the front door.

During this time I couldn't watch TV or listen to the radio. As the never-ending fever swirled in my head, all I could really do was lie still and just *be*. Going anywhere or having a life was out of the question.

Two books camped out on my bed—Louise Hay's *You Can Heal Your Life* and Bernie Siegel's *Love, Medicine and Miracles*. They were my bibles. I spoke affirmations to heal my body. I created an art journal and drew pictures of my insides. Bernie asked me if I wanted to live. I said, "Yes, Bernie, I do, I do." I drew healing rays entering me.

As I lay in bed day after day, I also felt the presence of angels as well as the love of everyone who missed me from the senior center where I worked. Or maybe it was just the fever. Either way, I sensed the presence of an extraordinary amount of light around me.

When I could hang out in the brilliance of this light, I could relax a bit. It wouldn't last for long, however. Soon I'd be asking myself questions like, "Will I be alive by the end of the day?" At this point, the doctors didn't know what was making me so ill, and just about every day I went into a state of overwhelming panic, afraid that I might die.

One day my friend Maxine called precisely when I was in one of those moments of terror. Maxine is one of those precious, sensitive souls with the ability to access deep inner realms. She helped me grow quiet and had me imagine a place in the Universe above and beyond the illness. With her gentle guidance, I was able to access this place, which felt timeless and full of love. Fear could not thrive in this realm. A deep sense of peace entered me. I was in touch with that which is Eternal.

Whenever I thought of this place, I could bring myself back to peace again. Unfortunately, I couldn't maintain it for more than a few days. Then I'd be back in the same old terror. And as far as yucky feelings go, terror is one of the worst. I needed something more.

Before the illness, I had been given a medium-sized, squishy teddybear that made a cute bed decoration. When I became sick, I found myself reaching for that little bear and hugging it a lot. Having this little stuffed thing tucked in my arms gave me a sense of comfort while going in and out of sleep, and in and out of fever.

One day a thought popped in: I wish I could give teddy bears to anyone who was going through an illness or lived with terror. I also wanted to share this deep feeling of comfort I felt with others who felt isolated or lonely.

When my sick leave from the senior center ended, I crawled back to work. One day, I mentioned the teddy bear idea to some of the grandmas at the center. They loved the idea. As a result, a project took shape. We became the "Seniors In Action Teddy Bear Crusade."

With tremendous support from the community, we collected close to a thousand teddy bears. Girl Scout troops and church groups donated bears. People holding garage sales gave us bears. And the seniors collected them too.

The local library held bear drives. They would advertise a teddy bear story hour and invite kids to bring bears for the project as well. The kids' parents loved the project because it encouraged their kids to give to others in need. The kids loved it, too. We'd bring three live humans costumed as bears and a group of seniors to join them for the story hour.

The three "live" bears: "Honey Bear"—a very boisterous, happy Pooh Bear, played by the cook at the senior center; "Bella Bear"—a polar bear with a pink ballet tutu and a big soft heart, played by one of the women who taught a class at the center; and "Papa Bear"—the "bear in a chair," one of the members of the senior center who was disabled and tooled around in an electric wheelchair, were always a big hit wherever we went.

We threw teddy bear tea parties for very ill children. We went to convalescent homes, hospitals, and centers for the developmentally disabled. After the big California earthquake in '89, the Red Cross contacted us and we sent bears to the kids who were living in the tent shelters in Santa Cruz after their homes had been destroyed. The local police department loaded the trunks of their patrol cars with bears that could be given to kids who were traumatized.

Wherever we heard of an individual in need, or a project who wanted us, we gave. Although I was still very weak, this project gave me a reason to keep on living. The act of giving gave me life.

One time we visited a center for brain-injured adults. One of the residents, a man in his early twenties, had sustained head injuries and lost an eye in a motorcycle accident. As Honey Bear gave this man a giant bear hug, he laughed and reached up to pet her big furry nose and talked to her.

The guy's therapist pulled me aside. "I can't believe it. He hasn't talked in six months or initiated contact with anyone since his accident." And here he was, happily engaged in contact and conversation with a giant Pooh Bear. The project ran for about three years.

Recently I donated some bears from my personal collection to children in an oncology ward in Bosnia. These kids had no toys. They didn't even have beds. They lay on cots in a sparse room. The bears wanted to go. They raised their little paws and volunteered. "Me. Me. Please send me." I always listen to the bears when they make such a request, and off they went on their very important mission.

If I had to experience such an intense illness, I'm glad that at least something worthwhile came of it: the teddy bears brought comfort and joy to lots of people. We shared our hearts and touched many lives. And a whole community rallied to put more love into the world.

Each life situation presents its own gift—although sometimes it is cleverly disguised.

~~~ Steps to Happiness NOW! ~~~

137) When God holds up a stop sign, take time out and take time in

Question: What's one of the quickest routes to "That Old Time Religion"—any religion or spiritual path? Answer: Illness. Let's face it—nothing inspires introspection or prayer and communication with God quicker than the anticipation of, or the diagnosis of, a serious condition. If you are ill, use this time to develop a deeper relationship with yourself and with your God.

138) Be easy on yourself

When I was sick, I put a lot of pressure on myself to heal. When I didn't get well immediately (or for a long time thereafter), I thought I'd failed. I had to learn that healing wasn't about failing or fixing. It was about being present and getting through each moment the best I could. I learned that I had to let go of all of the other moments and let them take care of themselves.

139) Look for the lessons

Illness can be a great teacher—so was Mrs. Linskey in third grade. If given my choice, I'd rather have chosen her. Nevertheless, I learned many lessons from being ill—one of which was that asking for help allows others the opportunity to give. If someone is able, available, and willing to give, it will make her heart feel good to do so. So let her.

140) When someone's ill, get real still

When someone is ill, one of the best things you can do for him is to be totally present and unconditionally loving. Hold a hand or lend an ear. Don't fill up the space with empty chatter. If you must talk, let your words be words from your heart, words of truth, words of love. Or just be present in silence. Often, it's your willingness to be there, more than your words, that makes the difference. Let your presence say, "I am here. I love you."

Enough Worms to Make Spaghetti

It's Story Time...

My friend Carol was out in her driveway picking up earthworms. She was not going fishing, however. It was pouring out, and she was rescuing them.

Although some of us might think this is a bit extreme, as Carol says, "Why should I leave them to drown when they can work for me?" Knowing Carol, even if they didn't work for her, she'd save them just because they were living things—slimy, creepy living things, but living things nonetheless.

Carol explained to me that when it rained hard, the ground would get so drenched that the poor little wormies would drown if they stayed underneath. So they'd come up to the surface to avoid drowning, only to die from exposure to the air, which dries their little bodies out.

Who knew wormies had it so tough? My memory of worms—yes, that one traumatic childhood memory—was of going outside after a rain to get my bike out of the garage, lifting the garage door, and discovering lots of worms, now all squished in the palms of my hands.

Just in case you were interested, my father's memory of worms was when he was a kid and he and his cousin had collected some to go fishing. All of sudden, their little cup of worms was missing. It turned out their younger cousin had put them all in his mouth to clean them off. Yes, this is a true story.

Pause for a moment. Any worm memories you'd like to share?

Meanwhile, Carol had just transported three hundred icky worms from her driveway to her giant flowerbeds, all of which were protected by an overhang, safe from the drenching downpour.

Next Carol went shopping. In the middle of the asphalt parking lot at Walgreen's, a single worm lay on the pavement. Carol found a clean styrofoam cup, put Mr. Wormy in it and left him on the passenger seat, and went about her shopping.

When she got back to her car, although the cup was there, Mr. Wormy had gone a-traveling and she couldn't find him. Finally, she saw him, lying face down in a dustball on the floor. He looked very dry, so Carol wet him. (Don't ask how. Actually I don't know how.) Then she drove him home and placed him in the flowerbed to meet his new friends. Another success story.

Carol has lots of success stories because she's rescued lots of things. For example, seventeen years ago she rescued a turtle named Agapanthus who still hibernates in her sleeping bag every winter.

She is also a mom to a beautiful, loving, old golden retriever found roaming on the streets after it had been given up for adoption, as well as enough cats for the neighbors to wonder about her.

For many months, she's also been playing Nurse Nancy to a very belligerent crow retrieved from the gutter after a nasty encounter with a car. For a long time, Beethoven the crow needed round-the-clock care and intravenous medications. He expressed his gratitude for her loving care by clamping down on her nose and leaving two big red tracks across her face while she was in the process of feeding him.

The turtle and the crow get along really well. Teensel, one of the cats, gets along with Beethoven, too. Not in the way you think. Teensel doesn't threaten or stalk the crow. They're just roommates, kind of like "the Odd Couple."

As if all this wasn't enough, every night Carol goes out at two in the morning to feed an opossum family which comes a-courting. One time, a blind opossum in very bad shape showed up at her doorstep. Of course, Carol fixed him up, and he joined the family, too. Every night he'd cuddle up in her arms as he drifted off to sleep.

Recently while buying some fresh corn at an organic grocery, she noticed some of the ears had caterpillars in them. So she went through the corn and picked out the ones with the prettiest caterpillars. She figured these were the ones that would make the prettiest butterflies. When she got home, she planted the sections of corn containing the caterpillars in little planters on her front porch and is waiting to see what happens.

Latest to join the family is a big white rabbit found in the middle of the road. "Bunny" and the cats have become best buddies as they chase each other up and down the hallway.

Of course, one of Carol's best rescues ever was me! When one of my more significant relationships headed for the afterlife, it was Carol who listened to my nights of endless wailing. It was Carol who supported me through those deep dark times. And it was Carol who encouraged me to spend time with animals so I could love again.

I am so thankful for this dear friend's presence in my life. So are all the other critters she's rescued—except for the crow.

"So, where's the spaghetti recipe?" you ask. I don't have one. It was just a metaphor. Making spaghetti out of worms is really twisted. Be kind to the worms and all the other icky, creepy, crawly things including the spiders with hairy legs. Be kind to all of them. Isn't that what we just learned in this story? Everything matters.

Animals are innocent and need your love—and sometimes, your help.

~~~ Steps to Happiness NOW! ~~~

141) Sometimes you have to rescue yourself

One time, Sluggo, my pet snail, was missing after Oshara cleaned out our fish tank. Devastated, we guessed he'd been accidentally poured down the bathroom sink with the waste water. An hour later, Sluggo crawled up out of the drainpipe. If Sluggo could rescue himself from a deep dark place, you can too. However, you may need to crawl through some slime.

142) If something's bugging you, you've gotta speak up

In spite of my futile attempts to swat them, seven flies buzzed around my kitchen. Most of them fumbled along the panes until they found the open window, except for one that I just couldn't get rid of. In exasperation I said to it, "If you've got so many eyes, how come you can't find the damned window?" whereupon it immediately flew across the room, found the open window, and sailed right out. See why it pays to speak up?

143) Value all life, including those with more legs than you

Upon discovering an unusual, multicolored spider in my bedroom and fearing it might be poisonous, I quickly captured it in a jar. I wanted to free it, but not around *my* house, just in case. So I chauffeured Mrs. Spider around town until I found an isolated spot to free her.

By doing this, I learned that practicing kindness, even toward insects and spiders, can make your heart happy.

144) When someone gives you a hand, don't bite it

My friend Debi works with vicious, fang-baring bobcats and ocelots. When they start baring their fangs and hissing at her, she responds by putting the back of her hand up to their noses. They, in turn, instantly respond by shutting their mouths and sniffing. Once they get her smell, they quiet down and allow her to give them their dinner. They know not to bite the hand that feeds them. Have you learned this lesson yet?

The Heart of Giving

It's Story Time...

I was en route to a comedy show when I saw a man on the busy street corner asking for money. On a bus bench next to him was a woman with a baby in her arms, and a two-year-old sitting quietly at her side. I passed by them and entered the lobby of the theater in eager anticipation of the performance ahead. For the next three hours, I was absorbed in the humor of the moment.

It was a little past eleven when the show ended. I was tired. It was late. Outside, the man on the street corner was still asking for money. By now the two year old was asleep on the cold, hard bench with his head resting in his mother's lap. The baby was asleep in her arms.

It tugged at my heart to realize this family had no place to go that night. I stopped to talk with them for a while, then gave them the few bucks I had. All that night and the next day, I couldn't get them out of my mind. Wasn't there something I could do? They were good people. They didn't deserve to be on the street. Although I knew I couldn't solve their situation, perhaps I could offer something to show that I cared.

I decided to bring them dinner. I baked a large chicken smothered with salsa, added ten baked potatoes, wrapped everything in foil, then drove the twenty-five minutes into the city.

I asked God to guide me back to that family. For the next forty-five minutes I circled the busy, bustling downtown area where I had last seen them. God must have been off playing golf somewhere because I couldn't find them.

I felt bad. But I still had this wonderful dinner in my car, and knowing the city was filled with hungry people, I decided I'd find somebody else to give it to.

Eventually I came to an empty lot where three or four homeless men were lying on the ground. They looked grubby and unshaven. At first I felt afraid. Were they too drunk to stand up? Maybe they were crazy. Having no idea what to expect, I rolled down my car window and said, "Excuse me, would you all care for a nice, hot, home-cooked dinner?"

They looked up in astonishment and were unbelievably grateful for the offer. One of them even volunteered, "We'll be sure to throw the paper plates and forks in the garbage when we're through. We won't throw them on the ground."

As I got back into my car, another said, "God's going to bless you for this."

And I replied, "And God will bless you too," then drove away.

My heart was soaring. I realized that when I had something to give, all fear dissolved. It felt so good to give. I could not be in my heart and be in fear at the same time. As soon as I was giving, the fear simply vanished.

A few days later, after attending a community function where there was a large supply of leftovers, I asked the event sponsors if I could take the food and find some people to feed. They agreed.

"Goody," I thought, "I get to go give some more!"

The next day I drove back to San Francisco and over to a park by the City Hall. A man sat stone-still on a bench, with a vacant look on his face. I could smell him from a distance. He smelled like cooked green peas, which smells great on peas, but not on people. At first, I was a little frightened to offer him food because again, I didn't know what to expect. Approaching him cautiously, I asked if he'd care for a sandwich.

His reply was so eloquent, I thought I was talking to an English gentleman.

"Why, yes, that would be lovely. What kind do you have?"

I opened the bag. He preferred tuna to egg salad and politely helped himself to a sandwich and some chips. As a parting gesture, he said to me in a way that felt both protective and caring, "You'll find that most people in the park are genuinely appreciative of such offers."

Next, I approached two men on another bench, and a woman who was lying face down in the grass next to them. The woman looked up bleary-eyed, her long black hair a mass of tangles. They took a bag of sandwiches, some chips and condiments, and said, "Thanks."

Next I saw an elderly woman sitting alone. When I offered her some sandwiches, she pointed a bony finger at me and emphatically stated, "Honey, the food is for the pigeons!"

"Oooookey-dokey," I said to myself, and moved on.

Giving out the last of the food, I headed back across the park to my car. As I was about to drive away, I saw something that brought tears to my eyes—the woman I had given food to earlier, the one who had been lying face down on the ground, was now going around to other people lying face down on the ground. She was waking them and offering them some of the food she had taken.

My giving had enabled someone else to give. And that touched me the most of all.

Love is the common denominator on this planet.

~~~ Steps to Happiness NOW! ~~~

145) Measure the success of your day by the love you've given away

I once met a woman named Gail Roberts who said, "As I go into this day, I ask, 'Where can I love?' Then I go and do a little love 'fluffing' here and there." The love in the Universe is as endless as the ways we have to express it. You never know what people are experiencing in their lives, so look at others through kind eyes. Smile. You might make the biggest difference in somebody's day.

146) The greatest safety lies within a loving heart

One cannot be in a loving heart and feel fear at the same time. It's impossible. When we give unconditionally, we truly feel good about ourselves. Whether it's through our work or a kindness of the moment, giving fills our hearts with wonderful twinkles. And there's nothing more fulfilling than a twinkle in your heart.

147) Angels are equal opportunity employers—so sign up

There's plenty of need for angels on this planet. So why not be one? Gather some close friends together and create an Angel Team. Decide how you're all going to be angels and just go do it. If you start from a place of joy, only more joy will come to you. And as you give of yourself, your heart will dance and your wings will begin to unfold.

148) God doesn't care about your ability or inability. God cares about your availability

So, how available are you? I don't know if we can change the whole world. I do know we can change the moment. Creating a positive change begins with one person—YOU—having one idea, setting one goal, and taking one action. You can make a significant difference if you open yourself to the possibility of doing so.

Wherever I Turn, Love Touches Me

It's Story Time...

Over the last ten years, as I made my annual pilgrimage to a synagogue for Rosh Hashanah and Yom Kippur, there was one man who always recognized me from the year before. He would greet me with a friendly hello and a smile of recognition. In a sea of strangers, I always felt welcomed by him.

At this year's service, I learned that over the past year he had died of AIDS. I didn't know he had been sick. In fact, I knew nothing about this man except that for the past ten years he had been friendly and kind to me in a setting where I often felt unseen and alone.

I thought about how this person, whom I'd hardly known, had touched my life. I wished I could have told him how much his welcoming eyes and smile had meant to me.

Back home, I sat down on my living room carpet and thought about his gentle and loving presence. As I saw this man in my mind's eye, I looked straight into his eyes. I didn't remember their color. However, I remembered they were beautiful and full of life. I felt his love coming to me. I kept looking at his face and the pure essence of his love continued to fill me.

I reached for my guitar and played some chords. I started hearing words. The song repeated itself over and over: "And I look in the faces of the ones I love."

I looked in this man's sweet face. I stayed there a long time, singing and feeling the continual outpouring and inpouring of love as I let the tears fall.

"And I look in the faces of the ones I love." I started looking directly into the eyes of my friends. I felt their love flowing back into me. As I felt how much they loved me, more tears fell.

"And I look in the faces of the ones I love." I looked into the eyes of everyone who had ever left me. They all looked back at me. I felt their love. In that second I learned that anyone who had ever left me, *had* loved me. Their truth was, they needed to go.

"And I look in the faces of the ones I love." I looked into the eyes of everyone in my family and felt how much I was loved by each of them.

"And I look in the faces of the ones I love." I looked into the eyes of everyone who had ever hurt me. All I saw was love. I saw the precious innocence of each soul.

I let the faces appear in my mind. There were so many. I realized how much I love people and how much I am loved. I realized I have always been loved. My heart felt cleansed as I released the flow of tears, just staying in the love.

"And I look in the faces of the ones I love." I challenged myself to look into the eyes of people I hate, including despicable characters in history. All I saw was love.

How was this possible? I didn't know why, and I didn't know how. All I experienced, though, was love. It felt as though I had gone beyond the human element, beyond the play of drama, of history, of cycles of abuse. My heart had gone so deep and was so open that all I could see and feel was love. Nothing outside of love could enter me. The facade of the personality, of all personalities, was stripped away. Everything had returned to its core, everything had returned to Love.

Recently I played the song again.

"And I look in the faces of the ones I love." Sitting alone on my living room floor, I imagined everyone I knew was sitting around me in a circle sending me love. I looked into their eyes. I sang the song, and they sang it back to me. They all had their hands up in front of them, sending me loving energy. I cried and cried. I felt so much love coming in.

I did that for a long time, and then I asked God, "Is there anyone else I need to see?" And the answer came back, "You."

I got out the floor mirror, picked up my guitar, cried some more and through the tears sang, "And I look in the face of the one I love." That was a biggie.

Sometimes when I'm in a grocery store or just see people walking down the street or whizzing by in a car, I sing this song to them. I don't sing it out loud. I sing it in my mind. It still counts.

I feel connected with everyone when I do this. Want to try it?

Look in the mirror. Send love to yourself. If you don't like what you see, change mirrors. Now look into the eyes of Love. They are your own.

Love is eternal; pain is not.

~~~ Steps to Happiness NOW! ~~~

149) Don't wait until you need surgery to open your heart

A woman with a reputation for treating her employees poorly recently underwent open-heart surgery. Upon hearing news of the surgery, one of her berated ex-employees proclaimed, "Looks like the only way they could open her heart was to do it manually." What does it take to open your heart?

150) Make the most of *This* day

When I was seven years old, I remember looking at a clock as the minute hand went around and realizing, "This minute will never come again. It's gone. And this minute will never come again...and this minute..." Each moment is precious. Time moves on, so make the best of your Now *now.*

151) Really get your priorities straight

I met a man whose wife was dying. Their lives had become an endless series of frustrating doctor's appointments and useless tests. One day toward the end, they played hookey on the doctors and drove to the ocean. Leaving her wheelchair in the car, he picked up his wife and carried her far down the beach. Nothing else mattered, except their time together and that beautiful day. It was a perfect farewell and a memory he treasures.

152) Wherever you go, the hearts will find you

If you are the kind of person who gives your best to others, the hearts will find you. You can go through the worst trials of life, but if you have a heart, the hearts will find you. Someone will come into your life. God will send him or her to you. The hearts will find you. You are never alone, so reach out. Talk to people. Talk to God and your angels. Speak your truth. The hearts will find you.

Final Thoughts

If you want to be happy:

Invite happiness to reside in your being. By welcoming happiness, you make way for magic and grace. In the place where magic and grace intersect, the creation of anything we want is possible.

Make joy your standard. Never settle for less.

Let go of the victim stance. God will not support us in being victims or in our whining, moping, or complaining about how hard, or unfair, or stressful, life is. Choosing to be a victim, or to whine, mope, or complain will only attract more opportunities for greater victimization. It's that simple.

Be as present in the moment as possible. If we can feel love in this moment, without judging ourselves or anyone else, or worrying about any other moment, our Now is going to be a lot happier.

Don't be attached to outcomes. We can block our good by thinking something needs to look a certain way. It doesn't.

Follow whatever positive flow is leading you forward. If nothing seems to be happening in spite of your best efforts, just be. Breathe. Observe. Grieve. Cry. Walk in nature. Meditate. Get clear.

Put your energy into that which sustains you. If you aren't feeling sustained at a financial level after you have done everything you can possibly do to find a job or create some form of alternative income, find something in your life that sustains you at a spiritual or creative level and ride that wave. We need to go with the flow and stay in our highest self possible, while believing that the other aspects of our lives will change in due course.

Take the next small step that's in front of you. If we think we should be further along, don't worry. We are just where we need to be in order to take the very next step.

Let go of that which you know is not for your highest good. We can never compromise the deepest parts of ourselves and create happiness.

Never withhold the truth from anyone for any length of time. If we speak our truth gently and with compassion, we will feel at peace. If we are afraid we'll hurt someone by telling the truth, we are supporting that person in living a lie until we speak up.

Push yourself to know the truth as well. There's a calmness in knowing the truth. Not knowing the truth always feels scarier than knowing the truth. When the unknown becomes the knowable, our fear often subsides.

If you want to be happy around your family, know your "PSP"—your "Parent Saturation Point"—and lovingly make your exit before you've reached it.

Disarm the "resentment monster." Any time we find ourselves being envious of others, we will make ourselves miserable.

Concentrate on something in your life for which you feel grateful. If you can't find one thing in life to be grateful for, grieve until you can feel gratitude again.

Develop "Chicken Consciousness," that is, keep your agreements with "im-PECK-ability." When you begin a sentence with the word, "I'll," that "I'll" stands for "I WILL." I WILL is a command. It is a statement of power. When we use this phrase, we are calling something into manifestation, so we need to make sure we really mean it. If we don't keep our agreements, the Universe will not take our requests seriously. After all, how can the Universe trust us to handle something bigger if we're not keeping our agreements at a smaller level?

Be open and willing to receive good. If someone offers you something positive, you need to say "yes" and accept it. If we do not accept the good offered to us in one area of our lives, we will block the flow of happiness in other areas. As we consider ourselves worthy of having happiness, the Universe will, too.

Maintain an unswerving commitment to create your dreams. We must not let anyone or anything deter us from achieving our heart's desires. If we feel discouraged along the way, we need to turn inward and listen to make sure that the pursuit of our dream is still what we want.

Allow yourself to feel all of your feelings.

Explore ways to express happiness. Pray. Love. Relax. Open to beauty. Sing. Dance. Give thanks. Praise. Rejoice.

Give up the notion of having perfect hair or the perfect body. There are only five people on the planet at any given time with perfect hair or the perfect body, and chances are, you and I are not among them.

Reach out to others. Each of us is called in our own unique way to serve a Greater Good. We might feel called to make a difference in the life of one other being, to serve at the level of our community, or to impact the lives of everyone on the planet. We are all here to be each other's angels. Give what it is that you want most to receive. After giving your best, let God do the rest.

Lastly, have patience and allow for God's divine right timing in order for your happiness to unfold. When doubt sets in, hold steadfast and believe that your prayers have been heard and that they will be answered. We must have compassion for ourselves. Things take time, but in the end, life always works out. Trust and have faith.